THE EXCEPTION

Other books by Susan Trott:

Pursued By The Crooked Man
Sightings
Don't Tell Laura
Incognito
When Your Lover Leaves . . .
The Housewife and the Assassin

for children:
Mr. Privacy
The Sea Serpent of Horse

THE
EXCEPTION
SUSAN TROTT

Carroll & Graf Publishers, Inc.
New York

First Carroll & Graf edition 1990

Carroll & Graf Publishers, Inc
260 Fifth Avenue
New York, NY 10001

Library of Congress Cataloging-in-Publication Data

Trott, Susan.
  The exception / Susan Trott. — 1st Carroll & Graf ed.
    p.   cm.
  ISBN 0-88184-626-0 : $17.95
  I. Title.
PS3570.R594E9   1990
813'.54—dc20   90-43551
                                                  CIP

Manufactured in the United States of America

to:
Phillip for the trails
Mujo for the path
Rita and Dick for being family

ONE

"Sister, did you see this in the paper about the Tragic Double Death?" I called to her in the voice she described as assured, bordering on imperious. I was in the kitchen, the *San Francisco Chronicle* in one hand, a spatula in the other.

"Yes. Isn't it sad?" she answered rhetorically from the dining room. Her voice was soft and slow, bordering on dejected.

"Horribly sad. The poor little kid," I muttered, more to myself. Now *I* sounded dejected.

Because we were orphaned, we were drawn to stories of families that lost parts of themselves, especially through violence, especially double deaths. Our dad died in a car crash on the Golden Gate Bridge which, celebrated for its beauty and romance, has fostered more violence than any other man-made structure outside of prisons and death camps. A month later Mom suicided off it.

"It's an unusual story," I said, still thinking aloud but also talking to Sister.

I'd just returned from a fifteen-mile run on the mountain in the pouring rain. I'd shed my wet clothes and wore Sister's long white terry robe. Half the time, if I'm not in running shorts, I'm in robes. I prefer the feeling of skirts to pant legs. Maybe I was a monk in another life, or a woman.

I was slugging down hot coffee as I read and cooked.

Sister was watching the rain, waiting for me to join her before eating her apple and muffin. She was just out of bed, still too groggy to wonder what she was going to do with her day and life—which, if she spent it like yesterday (and the last six months) would be nothing, for which she was beginning to hate herself.

I'd always known what to do with my day and life. Run. And be a Freeling. I was hopelessly literal and to me the fact that I was named Freeling was a statement of my position, and an affirmation. I was free to do exactly what I wanted with my life. (Everyone was but perhaps because of not carrying the legitimizing name, they didn't realize it.) I could choose my friends, dress any way I wanted, wear a pigtail, go to school only when and if I wanted, and every day just run like hell toward becoming the fastest marathoner in the world.

Yes, that's me, Boy Freeling. You may remember the name and you might have heard the tip of the iceberg of the story I'm going to tell, might have read it in the paper and mused aloud about it like Sister and I were doing about the double death.

It probably helped my ability to act like a freeling that my parents were dead and my sister, although conventional, adored me and didn't care what I did. Also, during my time of coming into my own, my high-school years, we'd lived apart—Sister being in college, I staying with a family friend in Sacramento named Ito, who was caretaker of a mansion there and took in homeless young people, especially obsessed young people who needed a place to practice. I thought of him as my real father. He was my role model.

"It's the old gun-cleaning story with a twist. I can't believe people really clean guns as much as they do. I can't believe so many people *have* guns." I sat down at the dining room table with my fried eggs, tomatoes, and potatoes surrounded by toasted sourdough bread and looked pityingly at Sister's icy cold and slim repast. "I will *never* have a gun."

Outside the window, limbs of drenched apple blossoms reached out and blended with a tall ancient bush of roses, a vase of which illuminated the table where we sat. Above the rose bush, which was pink, the gentle slopes of Mount Tamalpais were covered in cloud. The storm had subsided to an April shower and made a nice pattering sound on the windows and roof.

I experienced a moment of happiness. The run, the breakfast, the mountain that was like a family member. It was all so great. I felt so lucky. I wished Sister felt happy too.

"Do you have to clean a gun that hasn't been shot?" Sister asked.

"I don't know." I talked in between and during mouthfuls. "Anyhow, here the poor guy is, getting ready to clean his gun. He leaves the room for two seconds and his little stepdaughter comes in, picks it up, and kills herself. Three years old."

"He rushes to the room," Sister took up the tale. "And there's the little girl with a bullet in her head. Hard on his heels is her mother who heard the noise from the bedroom. The guy, who's only thirty himself, crushed by an insupportable guilt, completely unable to endure facing his wife's grief, picks up the gun and blows his head off."

I was silent, thinking how Sister so often used that

word "insupportable," which she got from Mom's suicide note. Then I asked, "Did he do right?"

"No!" Sister said. "Now she's lost two people. The two she loves most in the world. There is no one to comfort her in the loss of her child. Or in the loss of her husband."

Of course we couldn't help thinking about our own stunning loss four years ago. We'd comforted each other as best we could. At least she'd been old enough not to feel abandoned as deeply as I did. As I still do. They left us. They *chose* to leave us. Dad wouldn't have crashed if he hadn't been drunk. And Mom? Well, she just followed him, wanting to be with him more than with us, her children.

"The guy must have felt she would never forgive him," I said. "Maybe if it had been his child too, but it wasn't. It makes it worse."

"There's nothing worse than losing your child," Sister said.

"For me it would be to lose you," I said.

Sister said that wouldn't be true when I had my own family, whom I would necessarily love more than her. This, although it was years hence, seemed to make her feel more dejected. Me, too.

"Never," I said. "It's you and me forever. Orphans united!"

We got back to the story in the paper.

"We have to remember it's a gun-cleaning story, which we never believe," she said. "Whenever we read of a lone gun-cleaning story we *know* it's a suicide or a murder. So why would we believe this one? What does one *use* to clean guns with anyhow? A rag, some fluid or grease? It's so easy to put those items out afterward."

"It doesn't seem natural that the kid wouldn't have

just pointed the gun out in front of her instead of at herself."

"Maybe she was looking down the barrel to see what would come out."

We both fell silent at the poignant and ghastly picture.

I wondered why there'd be bullets in the gun if it was being cleaned. But I was losing interest now and reached for the sports page.

"It's so maddening that we never discover the truth," Sister said grouchily—which I liked to hear. Grouchy was better than blue. She'd been inspirited by the discussion. But then she said, "We never know," and slumped so far down she put her forehead to the table top. "The story fades and dies. We never know."

"So, become a policeman and find out. Or a psychic. You can be anything." She graduated from college in June, summered in Spain, returned home to stake out a life but, six months later, had only staked out a depression.

I, now eighteen, had staked out a life of winning the Boston Marathon at twenty-one. At twenty-three, I would set a world record at the Olympic Games. Simultaneously, I would matriculate off and on at Cal, studying philosophy and comparative religion.

Along with the house, we'd each inherited a college education, and sometimes, just when we needed it, we received money from a mysterious uncle, Mom's brother, who loved us in his mysterious way. Periodically, when his busy life allowed him to take time off from running the country (maybe the world) —or even when it didn't—he made an appearance in our lives. So, it wasn't just money he showed his love

with, it was time and attention, too. His name was
Masefield.

Having wrung the news story dry, I read the sports
and Sister resumed looking out the window. There
was only the sound of the gentle rain, my knife and
fork and, periodically, the plop of a camellia blossom
from the tree at the front of the house, hitting the
ground, unable to sustain the double burden of rain-
drops and decay.

Although I ate twice as much as Sister, we were the
same size: five feet six, one hundred and fifteen
pounds, which made her a fine figure of a woman and
me a sliver of a man. My hair was blond; Sister's was
light brown. We both had strong faces with dark eyes
and brows. My chin, however, tended to recede and
that, along with my large, sharp nose gave me an
avian profile. Yes, we looked alike except for my
blondness and except that she was beautiful and I was
ugly, if you thought of me as a man instead of a bird.
Of course, I wasn't fully grown and maybe my features would come right when I was. Certainly some
more pounds would benefit my appearance, but they
would hinder my speed—so that was out of the question. Whenever Sister or some friend asked me about
girl friends I always said, "Who would love a guy she
could see through?" and they had to agree—I was
that thin. My skin was translucently pale with such a
filigree of veins it was like looking at lace, and there
almost was the feeling you could see my organs, too.
Sister had the same milk-white skin, but on her it
looked lovely; it looked ethereal.

My given first name was Truman, but being literal
even as a youngster I found that unacceptable and
called myself Trueboy—occasioning gales of laughter
when I first stood up in kindergarten to give my name

to the class. Nevertheless, I imperturbably stuck by it and gradually, (mercifully, said Sister) it changed to Boy.

My name placed on me the onus of truth, but that was no problem. I had never lied and I never would. I was freeling and a boy of truth and that was how I was.

Sister's real name was Amy but because I called her Sister, everyone else did, too. She even introduced herself as Sister since by now she felt unconnected to her given name.

After breakfast, I did the few dishes, went out the back door through the laundry room where I tossed my muddy running clothes into the dirty wash basket, then stepped out across the boardwalk that connected Sister's back door to my front door. It crossed an artificial pond stocked with carp, the odd salamander, turtles and lilies. The boardwalk was a great place to Indian hand wrestle since the loser fell in the pond. This was Sister's sport. She took on all comers and never got wet—it didn't matter how depressed she was. She always won at her sport and yet I, the future Olympian, never had won at mine. I'd never even raced.

TWO

Our house was on four acres. At the front was a large lawn changing to field, sloping down to a young wood of oak, laurel, and madrone that skirted the redwood forest of the mountain. It was pretty fabulous. It cost peanuts when my folks had it designed and built but now, on the current Marin County market, it was worth millions. We kept it up ourselves. Sister shouldered the biggest burden of the work, but she enjoyed it.

My cottage, originally the servant's, consisted of one large room furnished with a table and three chairs, a single bed, a set of weights with a bench press, a couch and reading lamp, bookshelves. It had its own kitchenette and bath.

On one wall were pasted quotes from books and media mostly concerning persons similarly obsessed with one governing lifetime project. My latest was a quote from John James Audubon, taken from a book of his paintings. He said, "I never for a day gave up listening to the songs of birds, or watching their peculiar habits, or delineating them in the best way that I could."

This sort of remark brought tears of understanding to my eyes. "I never for a day," I murmured, throwing off Sister's robe and stepping into the shower, "gave up putting one foot in front of the other in the best and fastest way that I could." Never for one day.

"The trouble is that there may be ways of running I don't know about. It's time I got a coach. I don't want to. I believe I can do it myself. But I can't. That's arrogance, bordering on monomania. I've got to get a coach and start racing even if it means leaving home. It's one thing to know I'm fast. It's another thing to compete and prove it. I've got to start running with the big boys.

"Also I should go a day without running."

I had not missed a day of running for three years, two months, twelve days. This was a dangerous state of affairs because I was deathly afraid of the day I wouldn't run and would break my streak. The record had come to control me. It had a power over my life. It is hard to be obsessed and free at the same time, controlled and free. The fact is, for a freeling, I'm damned controlled and disciplined but the two can coexist. In fact, they have to. Otherwise, you'd have a man on a rampage—a tiny, ponytailed, see-through man on a rampage.

But I felt the record could destroy me if by some chance (hard to imagine what) I missed a day. There was almost a fear that I would go berserk. And yet, when I tried to force myself to miss a day and break the hold my streak had on me, I couldn't.

Ito, with whom I'd lived the four years Sister was in college, once told me, "It's fairly easy, Trueboy, to tell the truth, but it's hard to live the truth, to have the truth be in you."

Why did I remember that now while thinking of my unbroken daily record? And what did it mean, really? I shrugged. Ito's words seemed sometimes to haunt me so that I would have to shrug them off. I knew Ito loved me and believed in me and yet, when I remembered his words, they sometimes seemed to come as warnings, rather than as tokens of love and belief.

"I never for one day gave up listening to the song of birds . . ."

How beautiful that was. Audubon understood. Audubon was constantly paying attention to what mattered most to him. And so was I, Trueboy, paying attention. I simply should consider it as my normal daily life, rather than distinguishing it as a streak. Running is the same as eating, as breathing. Running is just breathing harder.

I pulled on clean jeans and a T-shirt, wound my braid into a toreador's knot, and set off for the Cactus Cafe, where I had a job as cook during the lunch hours. I drove an old Volvo that had been Dad's hack-about car—not the car he crashed.

The Cactus was a hole-in-the-wall Mexican restaurant next to a liquor store overlooking a parking lot. Despite its prickly decor, it was cheerful inside and the food was healthy and tasty. I started work at eight-thirty to prepare for the eleven o'clock opening. This meant I boiled the chicken, roasted the peppers and eggplants, cooked pinto beans, washed lettuce, and so on.

As I got out of the Volvo, there in the parking lot, about to get into his pickup, was Ito, whose words I'd been haunted by in the shower. Half Samoan, half Japanese, he was a big man growing steadily bigger since his marriage. He looked like a professional wrestler. If you asked him what he did, he'd say he was a gardener, which was true. He probably wouldn't tell you he was a Zen Buddhist priest.

He was a wild card Zen priest who came and went

from the Zen community. Sometimes he would lecture at the San Francisco Zen Center or at Green Gulch, but he felt he had nothing to say and after a while would get disgusted with himself for thinking he did.

Although he was the soul of gentleness and goodness, he had a fierce and uncompromising delivery which made the other Zen lecturers seem cute and anecdotal, almost kittenish. Afterward, the congregation, instead of smiling and chatting together, staggered out as if hit by a sledgehammer, all going off in different directions to be alone with themselves, like pool balls after the break.

Whether Ito spoke or didn't speak, I thought as I walked over to him, Ito was a man one felt good just standing next to, just being in the same room with, the same parking lot, world.

"Ito!"

"Boy!"

We hugged each other, I disappearing into his embrace, being about the size of one of his arms.

We exchanged news of our lives since we'd last visited then I said, "Ito, this is so great that I ran into you because I have just decided it's time to take off, find a coach, and get serious. I wouldn't have gone without saying good-bye. I'll want your blessing."

Ito looked at me, taking in my person, my stance, my heart, my dream. He nodded. Someone else might have thought the nod was absentminded but I understood that I had his blessing, the boon of his understanding and approval, even though I was not choosing the path of the dharma, the way of the sage.

To be driven by ambition, to have a gigantic, fanatical goal to be the best and to be acknowledged as such—this is not Zen. Ito didn't care. He loved me. He understood.

"I'm scared," I admitted. Saying it, I realized the truth of it. Being by Ito brought to the surface the "truth that was in me."

"That's good." Ito smiled. He nodded again.

Twice blest! I exulted.

THREE

While I cooked up a storm at the Cactus, Sister continued to sit lethargically at the dining table, head in hands, elbows on the classified section advertising jobs available, watching the rain. She'd come back from Spain with a high heart, thinking to get a job in San Francisco in public relations or advertising, but every firm she went to was a turn-off. She looked at the employees and thought, I do not want to be with these people every day. I do not want to be *like* these people. This gave her a scornful countenance and made the people she didn't want to be with not want to be with her either.

She didn't know how to type, proceeding under the theory that if she didn't know how to she wouldn't have to. This was not a viable theory. The few interesting jobs she came across required typing. She got temporary jobs filing or being a receptionist. She tried selling, but it was intolerable to stand in one place all day. It was just as intolerable to sit or walk around. Lying down wasn't bad. But it didn't go anywhere, didn't take her life forward. In fact, there was a definite feeling of going backward, all the way to the womb.

Now she'd fallen into a futile period of not even looking for a job. She thought she would be creative during this fallow time, develop photographs she'd taken in Spain, write some poems, make some clothes, learn to type. But she didn't do any of these things; she watched the rain or, if there was sunshine, lay down in it, preferably naked. There was at least a feeling of accomplishment accompanying the minute darkening of her pale, pale skin.

The truth was, she was happiest simply staying home, keeping the house and herself looking nice. She found such chores intensely pleasing and, on an even lower level, was so charmed to sit quietly, as she was doing now, with not an idea in her head. But it made her feel horribly guilty.

She was young, smart, good looking, had a B.A., and had always been disciplined and hard working. What was the matter with her?

She looked at the rain wondering why she was such a failure.

I'll wash my hair, she thought, pushing away the unscanned paper, running her hands through her chic short cut that was like a long crew cut, standing straight up from her forehead, light brown and shiny. *That will cheer me up. And I'll paint my nails.* She looked down at the pearly pink perfect ovals of her nails. She had painted them yesterday—also washed her hair. *And after that,* she vowed, *I'll watch the rain some more. Somebody's got to watch it.*

When she emerged from the bathroom, wearing towels on body and head, scowling because Boy had taken her robe, she found Uncle Masefield sitting in the living room. Her heart pounded with excitement and surprise.

He stood up and greeted her with a smile and the quiet utterance of her name, "Sister."

"Masefield! How great!" But her heart sank. It was

not great for him to find her thus, a lowly showerer and rainwatcher—she who'd shown such promise.

He was a man in his mid-forties: tall, dark, quintessentially cool. His face was engraved with lines, but he looked young and handsome to Sister and to every woman. He had the family white skin, but his hair was black and curly and his eyes were that uncanny violet color that one in a million get as a prize for being a hero in another life, or for going to be a hero in this one.

He did something important in Washington; no one knew exactly what, but there was the feeling that without him there, things would be even worse. In truth he was rarely there—he was a citizen of the world. He knew everything there was to know about politics, affairs of state, affairs international. He had twice declined cabinet positions—not only for different presidents, but for different parties. When he was Sister's age, he'd been a spy, been caught, spent time in Siberia.

He looked at his watch.

"Won't you be late for work?"

She flushed painfully.

"Still no job, eh?"

"Right. Do you want some coffee?"

"Yes, please." He leaned against the kitchen counter while she poured. No one could lean against a counter like Masefield, Sister thought. His "cool" was indescribable. All those metaphors of wild cats in repose didn't do the job, she thought. If you could imagine a man leaning against a counter who fully realized that he was the smartest, most irresistible person in the world and, on top of that, immortal, you'd begin to get the idea.

"What do you want to do?" Masefield asked her gently.

"I don't know." Sister started to cry and was mortified. "I don't even know," she wailed softly.

He took the coffee from her trembling hand. She wiped her eyes and nose on the towel that was draped on her head.

"Of course, you don't. Why the hell should you? Up until now, your months, nights, and days have been scheduled for you. You've always known what was coming up next. Suddenly you're on your own and you haven't the slightest idea how to proceed."

Sister was thrilled to be understood, but his empathy made her feel more emotionally frail. She had to restrain herself from throwing herself onto his chest and sobbing her heart out.

"It's a passage," he went on. "But it's an unacknowledged passage. Instead of your tribe throwing a wild passage party with all-night dancing, strong brew, incantatory songs, and bloody mutilations to ready you for the next phase, they just maddeningly ask you if you've found a job yet, right?"

"Yes, and here's Boy, four years younger, who knows exactly what his whole life is going to be. I don't even know what to do with the next minute."

"I was the same as Boy. My motto, gleaned from Ecclesiastes was: *'Whatsoever thy hand findeth to do, do it with all thy might . . .'* "

"But my hand can't findeth anything!" Sister interrupted.

"Go get dressed. I have an appointment for you in San Francisco."

An hour later they parked in front of a faded yellow Victorian on the back side of Pacific Heights in San Francisco, a region the realtors liked to call

"Lower Pacific Heights," as if it were a continuation of the amazing mansions above instead of the beginning of the crime and sleaze section.

There was a bronze plaque beside the door that proclaimed the business: Roommates, Inc.

"Walk in there and say you want a job. When he asks if you can use a computer, tell him the truth but tell him you're a quick study. Tell him you're smart and intuitive, good at languages, a hard worker. All of which is true, in case you've forgotten."

"What if he offers me the job but I don't want it?"

"If he offers you the job, take it, see how it goes."

"All right." Sister tried not to sound hopeless and ended by sounding mournful.

"When you're in a period of not knowing what to do, it's good to do something, anything, until the right thing reveals itself. The right thing isn't going to come to your front door. You have to get out there in the world where it can find you."

"You came to the door, Masefield."

He smiled. "Yes, I came to the door."

They smiled at each other. Sister didn't want to get out of the car. She didn't want to leave Masefield's side. He was a hard man to leave the side of. She wished she was his daughter. Or she wished she could marry him. He never had married, but she knew there was a woman in his life with whom he'd had a child he honored as his son.

"Tell me the rest of the Ecclesiastes quote."

He said it gravely, sonorously, almost lovingly. *". . . do it with all thy might for there is no work, nor device, nor knowledge, nor wisdom, in the grave wither thou goest.'"*

She grimaced. "Oh, great." The quote absolutely terrified her.

"When you think about it later, you'll realize it's life-affirming. It will make every minute precious." He reached across and opened her door. "Ito says that the Buddha says suffering is a characteristic of life."

"Am I suffering?"

"Yes."

It cheered her up. It made her feel less guilty. Suffering sounded so much more noble than being depressed, and the Buddha himself had said she was not alone in this.

"You probably delayed your anger and grief about your folks," he said. "That, combined with *the passage,* threw you down and put a hammerlock on you. But now, my advice is to get going again."

She stepped out of the car, wrenching herself away from the spell that he cast. It had stopped raining.

She went up the wooden steps. When she turned to wave to Masefield, he was gone.

FOUR

Sister remained a moment in waving position, her hand still in the air, as her eyes hectically searched for the disappeared Masefield. Then she turned to face the door of Roommates, Inc.

Walk in, said a small sign. She did. There was a waiting room with benches around three walls, no one sitting on them. Knock, said a sign on the next door. It was like Alice in Wonderland.

"Come in!" A boyish voice.

The interior room was bright and bare with one chair, a desk which supported a computer and printer, no filing cabinets, no pictures. It didn't look like much of a going concern. The words "fly-by-night-operation" came to Sister's mind.

"Yes?"

He was freakily tall and fair and looked, she thought, from her own lofty age of twenty-two, hardly out of his teens. He wore a white button-down shirt and new, dark blue Levi jeans. This was, to Sister, acceptable garb were it not that, instead of the customary topsiders, sneakers, or loafers, he wore some clumsy depression-era work boots reminding Sister of a photo by Walker Evans. Maybe they didn't make normal shoes big enough for this kid?

"I've come to apply for a job. Here's my resume."

He looked at her resume and then he looked at her. His eyes seemed violet, too. Masefield must have left her in a violet haze. She blinked and shook her head.

"Can you use a computer?" he asked.

She answered as Masefield had instructed. When he remained silent she added the other things he'd told her to say. "I'm hard working, good at languages, and intuitive." She left out smart, feeling that should be evident.

"Intuitive?" he laughed. He had long, flexible lips that curled up at the ends. He was almost as blond as Boy. "That's a funny thing to say while applying for a job." He laughed again. "Intuitive." He seemed to think it was hilarious.

Sister began to feel angry. Still, her pissed-off look was an improvement on the scornful one she previously had brought to job interviews.

The feeling was aggravated when he said, "What kind of a name is Sister? Is this a real name—Sister?"

She flushed. "My name's Amy, but Sister's what I've been called for so many years, it seemed ridiculous to put down a name I wouldn't answer to."

"Well, it's time to hang up the nickname. It completely diminishes and unsexes you."

"If you are considering me for this job," Sister said coldly, "I'd like to know more about it." She didn't know why she said "more" since she didn't know anything except that it was probably fly-by-night and run by a kid who still should be in school.

But Boy should be in school and wasn't. Maybe the people who got on in the world didn't go to college and then didn't have to go through the hated "passage." She didn't know why Masefield even called it a passage, which meant it went from one place to another, when what she was in was a hole.

He went into a job description during which he stood up and sat down again several times, and she saw that he was at least six five but his frame was delicate as were his features. If a person that tall could be said to look feminine, he did. His face was so sensitive it made hers feel carved in stone. When he talked, all his features moved, even his nostrils.

"Nowadays," said he, "housing is so expensive people have to team up and those new to the city have no friends to share with. Some people have no friends anyhow. We try to match people. Our computer stores information as to who has housing and who's looking for it. Customers fill out questionnaires telling as much as possible about themselves. Still, we have to use our *intuition* as to who might be gay, or a mental case, or a troublemaker. Any intuitive info we add to the persons file, but in a way that it won't print up on the readout. It costs them twenty-five dollars to sign up with us and another twenty-five dollars when we find them a roommate. I'll pay you ten dollars an hour if you want the job."

"I'll take it," Sister said, only because Masefield had told her to. She added wryly, "Do you think you can buy me a chair to sit on?"

"I like to keep the overhead down. There's a certain amount of footwork to the operation, too, so we won't be here together that much."

"Why aren't any customers here now?"

"We're closed Monday and Tuesday, open on weekends."

"Oh great, I have to work weekends?"

"Right. I suppose you know that you have an attitude problem."

She stifled a retort. He was right. Realizing this made her want to cry for about the fourteenth time that day.

"Want a ride home?" he asked.

"I live in Mill Valley," she said dauntingly.

"So I saw on your resume. I hope you don't mind motorcycles. I've got an extra helmet."

Sister had no history to know if she minded motorcycles, and soon was torn between terror and exhilaration as she was carried up, over, and dramatically down Pacific Heights, then across the Golden Gate Bridge (which she didn't blame for her parent's deaths), down the Waldo grade and along the bay shore, through town, up a narrow winding road and down a gravel driveway to her sprawling house of shingled redwood and glass.

Only when she saw his expression did she remember what an architectural knockout it was to someone seeing it for the first time. It had been a while since someone new had visited.

He followed her in, pausing to look appreciatively at the vase of roses ("Flowers!" he said. "I love flowers!), the now-clear mountain view, then all around the spacious light-filled rooms.

"This place is huge! Do you have a roommate?" At her negative, he cased the house, going from room to room in Bunyanesque strides.

Sister sat down on the living room couch, happy to be home, but feeling her depression returning to nibble at the edges of her psyche.

She wished she hadn't taken the job. What would she tell people—that she was working for a teenager finding roommates for the friendless until her boss flew in the night? What was the future in such a job? Still, she'd promised Masefield. For Masefield, she'd do anything. Whether she'd do it with "all her might" was doubtful.

"You could get four hundred dollars renting out the extra bedroom. Do you want a roommate? I'll be your roommate."

"Are you a mental case? A troublemaker? Are you gay?"

"No to the first two questions, probably yes to the last. I haven't had a sexual relationship, but my feeling is that I don't like women. I like men much better. They're more . . ." he paused, ". . . like me!"

Sister perked up, felt warmed by his admission. "But that's natural at your age. I mean, what are you, seventeen?"

"I'm twenty," he said. "Speaking of gay mental cases, there goes one walking by your house right now."

Sister joined him at the window. "That's my brother."

"Ah! The brute who saddled you with the name of Sister?" He looked after him, pondering. "He certainly is a tiny brute. You could have withstood him. You could have said leave my name alone."

She turned away. His rudeness really made her mad. At the same time there was something intensely likeable about him.

"By the way, Amy, how did you happen to come looking for a job at Roommates, Inc. ? The reason I ask is," he gestured at the classified section on the table, "I didn't advertise. In fact, there wasn't a job available, but when you walked in asking for one, I thought, why not? I can use an intuitive sidekick."

Sister felt reluctant to tell him her uncle had taken her there. It sounded pathetic, as if she had no get-up-and-go—which was the truth.

She evaded the question. "What's your name by the way? I don't even know who I'm working for."

"M Scott," he said. "As in the letter M," he responded to her puzzled look.

"Are you kidding? You hector me about my nickname and yours is *completely* a diminutive!"

"Hey, we're talking capital M here, not small. But okay, fair enough. If you take on Amy, I'll take on my full name right now." He staggered as if the idea gave him a heart attack. "No, I can't. I'm not up to it. You see, I'm named after my incredibly illustrious father and I'm only worth one letter."

"Come on," Amy smiled. "Try!"

He straightened his shoulders, stood tall, which was really high. "Maybe I'll go half the distance, which for me is a giant step toward autonomy. Masef," he said. "Masef. Yeah, I like it." He grinned.

He noticed she was smiling at him for the first time, transforming from her previous sullen self to a glorious shining woman, a stunning beauty. She was throwing herself into his arms, crying, "Cousin!"

He extended his smile to each ear and hugged her back. "So Dad sent you to me. I'll be damned. Masefield works in quiet ways, his wonders to perform. So, you're the mystery orphans always held up to me as children who overcame tragedy to become superior people: Boy a future Olympian, Amy a future chairman of the board. Whereas I, despite being loved and cared for on all sides, grew too tall for one thing, dropped out of school for another, and can't hold down a job for more than a month at a time."

"And you're the mystery son of whom I've always been jealous because Masefield loves you so much more than me or Boy," said Amy, smiling away, experiencing happiness for the first time in months.

"That's right. He does love me a lot, even though I'm such a loser."

"If you're a loser and I'm working for you, what does that make me?"

"Chairman of the board. See," he expanded his arms like semaphores, "already you've fulfilled your destiny. We'll get cards printed up tomorrow. And I'll tell you what the job really is. It's awfully nice work. Which one is my room? I want to go and claim it. When can I move in?"

"Help yourself," Amy said, "but first come and meet Boy. We go out the back way, across the board-walk. Follow me."

He followed, wondering at the sudden, fleeting maniacal expression that had cruised across her features.

Oh good, she said to herself, feeling as Masefield had promised she would, the preciousness of the moment, thinking how there was no hand wrestling in the grave wither they'd be going, but there was as much as she wanted now and, she remembered (How could she have forgotten?), that it was more fun than almost anything. *I can't wait to throw him in the pond.*

FIVE

From my cottage window, I saw Sister bring Masef across the boardwalk ostensibly to meet me, but really to show him that becoming a member of our household wasn't that easy. First, he had to pass through the crucible: the Indian hand wrestle. I listened and watched through the open window.

"Do you know how to Indian hand wrestle?" she asked casually.

"Sure."

"Let's."

"Okay. But watch out," he said confidently, "I was taught by a real Indian, my best friend, Laurie."

Standing opposite each other, they put their right feet flush together, right hands linked, thumbs up and pressed together. "Hey," he said, looking at her nice outfit, "there's water on each side."

"That's all right." Sister passed a finger through their thumbs, which was the signal to begin.

He loomed above her. She was used to fighting with me, a person of her own height and weight. I watched, trying to learn her secret because it annoyed the hell out of me that she always won when I was twice as strong and ten times the jock.

Pushing her hand toward him then jerking it to the left, she immediately unbalanced him. He wavered,

one leg off the ground, looking like a great blue
heron trying to rise into flight with only one wing.
Then with a howl of defeat and a mighty splash, he hit
the pond.

"Rematch!" he cried desperately, just as I always
did, blundering out of the water like the creature
from the black lagoon. "Two out of three!"

Three years went by.

Young Masefield, previously M, now Masef ("Pro-
nounced," he instructed his friends, "massive.") did
come to live with me and Sister, now Amy, but she
did not charge him any rent because he was her
cousin. He was family. Family meant a lot to her; she
had so little of one. He shared expenses and motorcy-
cled her to and from work. He was easygoing, liked
to play classical guitar (we could not tell how well but
it sounded nice) as much as he liked to shoot baskets
with his buddies, or lie in the sun, or watch movies.
He seemed to be able to do absolutely nothing of any
importance for lengths of time without being depressed or bored or guilty, and Amy observed this
with interest.

Masef and I (Massive and Tiny, Masef liked to say,
or Adult and Boy) had a grudging fondness for each
other but, maybe because of my being so literal, I
couldn't handle Masef's breezy teasing-type humor,
his joking. Joking, to me, is a way of evading what
you're really feeling or thinking. Sister says it's just
another way of communicating, providing a mode to
say things that are difficult. In any case, since I was
soon off on my quest to learn more about running,
how I got along with Masef didn't matter and I was
glad to leave Sister in good hands.

Masef, being an only child, was amazed to witness

our farewell: Sister and I shedding tears, repeating countless times, "I love you. I'll miss you," while exchanging promises to think about each other every day. Of course, it wasn't just that we were brother and sister—it was that we were orphans.

"Orphans united!"

"Forever!"

We wrote and called each other constantly the whole time we were apart. Periodically, I revisited.

Roommates, Inc. turned out to be a subrosa organization finding housing and work for Mexican, Central American, and South African refugees—now oddly called aliens. It also provided for any first worlders who walked in off the street. They supported the business along with a mystery grant, probably from Masefield. It was good work. Amy's depression was soon dissipated and she flourished.

True to her first feeling about the operation, its owner did fly in the night, leaving her sole proprietor, but with a going concern. Masef had said she might find him suddenly gone one morning but not to worry, he would return. During the three years, he appeared and disappeared six or seven times.

On the occasion of his first return—after being four months gone—Masef and Amy were so happy to see each other, they fell into each other's arms and into Amy's bed and Masef into Amy. It was not as fast as all that, more of a dance than a collision, but unexpected, involuntary.

Afterward, they lay tightly together as if fastened but afraid (Masef terrified) to look into each other's eyes. *Maybe she's dead from this,* he thought, holding her tighter and, indeed, crushing the breath out of her. *At least if she's dead, I won't have to look into her eyes. They won't be there.*

"Masef!" Amy gasped. "I can't breathe!"

"I'm sorry, Amy. I don't know what I'm doing. Or what I did. Are you all right? I think I lost my virginity, Amy. Did I bleed?"

"Don't joke, I feel too emotional. Too . . . stunned. Too . . . happy I guess. Are you happy?" Now she looked at him, he at her. Both their flawless young faces were expressionless with the wiped-slate look of sexual satiety and subsequent divine repose. Yet Amy said, "I don't think you are happy."

"We're cousins and I'm gay. It makes this a bad idea." He unloosened his body from hers and lay back in a sprawl as if he'd been dropped from the ceiling. Bad idea or not, he began to smile. "So this is sex," he said, smiling away.

"You're not gay."

"I'm pretty sure I am. I hate women."

"You don't hate me!" Her voice squealed slightly at the outrageousness of the notion.

"It's because of my mother."

"Do you hate your mother?"

"No, I love her. But a man died because of loving her and I guess it left me feeling that if you love a woman, your life won't matter anymore—not to yourself and least of all to her."

At this Amy had a flickering, glancing remembrance of the gun-cleaning story, the tragic double death. It surfaced like a flying fish catching a ray of sun then disappearing, leaving the viewer wondering what she'd seen.

"Oh, Masef, I'll cherish your life," she vowed with all her heart. "I'll never let any harm come to you."

He looked at her wide-eyed, "What a wonderful

thing to say. I'm so touched. What a dear person you are." They were silent, then Masef added, "There's a girl named Laurie who I've loved all my life and who loves me in return."

The Indian girl, Amy remembered.

"But I never felt sexy about her. Once I tried to make love to her, but I couldn't. This would kill her." He gestured widely, encompassing the two of them on the bed. Through the window, the sun made a similar gesture, breaking through a cloud to highlight the scene, since in their pell-mell rush toward union the curtains hadn't been pulled. "I told her it wasn't to do with her or my love for her—it was because I was gay. That way she wasn't hurt by my marked, even arresting, nonarousal. Now this! This dazzling non-nonarousal."

Amy remained silent, only shifting her body closer to his. *What long arms and legs he has,* she thought, *even a long neck. It's like being in bed with a giraffe.*

"We grew up like brother and sister," he said, as if quoting someone. "Our mothers were best friends and suckled us interchangeably."

After a while Amy said, "I have to tell you that although I've had lovers, until now the only man I've ever loved, in a fantasy way, is your father."

"No wonder you called out Masefield instead of Masef while in the throes of passion. I thought that was fishy."

"I never did!"

"Let's try again and see if you say my name right this time. How is it you do this thing? It was all so quick and unexpected, I didn't pay attention. What was the connection point—belly buttons? Ankles?"

Amy giggled "First we kiss. It's important to have a lot of kisses interspersed with saying nice things about the person. Then you move along very gradually . . ."

"You mean it doesn't *always* take thirty seconds."

Amy showed him how long it could take. He was a quick study at slowness. They had a wonderful time and they remained faithful, adoring lovers all during the next years, even with Masef's erratic arrivals and departures. He also became equally good at hand wrestling so they had wonderful competitions at which, when meeting after a long absence, it was a toss-up whether to hand wrestle or make love. It had reached another dimension whereby, after the signal to begin, they would stand together minutes at a time, feet together, hands linked, eyes locked, not moving, waiting for, trying to create, the psychological moment of imbalance—before setting it in motion. Tantric hand wrestling. And so also did their lovemaking achieve long, endless immemorial moments of only looking into each other's eyes—they who had been so afraid to look at first.

SIX

During the three years Amy saw Masefield, too.

Although her visits with her uncle were always brief, there was ever the wrench at parting, always the feeling she would go with him if she could, stay with him, marry him if he would have her. It was upsetting to her especially because of loving Masef. She couldn't know that other women felt the same, men too. He had charisma, a power that was like magic. Masef felt it but supposed it was just because he so passionately loved and admired his father.

Masefield did not abuse this innate power because to him it was nothing compared to the power he respected and sought, which was knowledge. He was a man who wanted to know why the world wags and what wags it. His life was a matter of being curious about things, finding them out and then, if possible, changing the course of history with his findings. He was a great believer in interference.

Because Ito, his best friend, believed in noninterference as a tenant of Zen Buddhism, they had many arguments, neither budging. "If you sit back and let things happen, Masefield said, "you're only allowing someone else to interfere, someone dumber than you, with less understanding, less of a handle on the facts."

"Playing ball together in the fields—two people, one heart."

"Typically, you propose an image to avoid discussion," Masefield grumbled. "I suppose it is an image of two persons without agendas. However, I don't believe in happenstance, I believe in individual designs. Someone is always pulling the strings. Everyone has an agenda. Now, if a man were in a lake . . ."

"And he happened to be drowning and I happened to be passing by I would save him," Ito replied, also grumbling. The two friends, unlike as they could be, always fell into the same tone when talking together. "And I'm tired of the lake. You bring it up every time. Nonattachment doesn't mean not giving a shit."

Because Masefield, over the years of his unclehood, had established a precedent of coming and going, disappearing and reappearing with never an explanation, Amy never questioned Masef's absences, only assumed they were, in the spirit of his legendary father's, required and probably important. They weren't.

It was from Laurie she learned how unimportant his absences were.

Yes, she met Laurie, the woman Masef had loved since he was born. It was in the third year of this story.

By now, Amy had passed on Roommates, Inc. to a friend, just as Masef had passed it on to her, and was happily working as a photographer for the local paper, with a small start-up, side business of portraits.

That was why she was home in the middle of a weekday when Laurie appeared out of the blue. She came to the door, which as usual was wide open, and shouted, "Anybody home?" When Amy appeared, she introduced herself. "I'm Laurie Scott."

Amy was confused, then recollected, "Masef's Laurie? Come in," she said warmly. "I didn't know you had the same last name."

"We do. We're both bastards, you know."

Amy hadn't known.

"M took his mother, Sunny Scott's, last name when she didn't marry Masefield. When my mother married Sunny's father, Muir Scott, he adopted me."

Laurie was tall and strong looking, with thick, glossy black hair to her shoulders. Her face was dark-skinned and kind of mean looking. She didn't look like a woman you'd want to mess with, that you'd want to, say, be in the position Amy was in of being lovers with her childhood sweetheart. She hoped Laurie didn't know.

"Come on in," she repeated. The house entrance was to an enclosed porch, "highly windowed," as Masef said. It was painted white, even the floor, and strewn about with green wicker lounges and chairs with Hawaiian print cushions. It was the preferred area, over the living room, except for a few months in winter when it was too cold and the fireplace wooed them to the living room. The other main gathering places were the front lawn and around the dining room table.

Amy went no further than the porch. She took a chair, but Laurie didn't follow suit. Her stance struck Amy as confrontational. Now she wished she hadn't sat down, although Laurie would tower over her either way. She wished she could hand wrestle her for Masef, winner take all, since she'd win. Then they could just get on to the business of being friends.

"I know about you and M being lovers. He didn't tell me. Masefield did."

Why the heck had he told? Had it "killed her,"

Amy wondered, remembering Masef's fears along this line, forthrightly expressed after their first love-making, fears which had been repeated many times over the years accompanied by anguished, almost hunted, expressions.

Amy thought Laurie looked as though she was surviving the knowledge. Except for looking mean, which was probably habitual.

"He didn't tell me where you lived. I found that out for myself."

She seemed to expect a response. Amy said, "Oh."

"I think you should know a few things about M."

Amy, in her own way, could be a woman not to mess with. "Thanks, Laurie," she said. "I'd just as soon learn about Masef on my own experience of him." Yes, Amy could lay things on the line—the only difference was she flushed at the same time. And trembled. She reckoned Laurie wouldn't flush or tremble.

Laurie's black eyes raked Amy's face. "Do you have anything to drink around here? Like a beer?"

"Yes." It was a relief to get out of the chair. "Sorry not to have offered sooner," she said genuinely, feeling remiss in her hospitality, although a beer wouldn't have occurred to her at this hour of the morning.

They went to the kitchen, Laurie looking around the house as if deciding where to start burning it down.

"How long since you've seen M?" she asked Amy.

Amy pondered whether to answer. She ran her hand through her hair which was longer now, curly and sunstreaked, frothy-seeming next to the dark, shimmering weight of Laurie's.

"A month, right?" Laurie answered for her. "I

know because he comes to see me when he leaves you."

Amy shrugged, thinking, this woman's so jealous she can't see straight. She pulled the cap off a Pacifico and passed her the bottle. She'd be the type who drank out of the bottle, Amy figured, then she'd eat the glass afterward.

Laurie took a long draught, head tilted back. She had beautiful skin, Amy noticed. Incredible muscle tone. An athlete. Probably some murderous event like putting the shot.

"After he sees me," Laurie went on, her eyes pinned to Amy's white face, "he goes travelling, no one knows where. He hits the road. Not for any reason. Not to do anything. Not even to see the world. I'd say it's just to get away. Right now, from you." Her eyes glinted.

Amy shrugged again. She hoped it wasn't developing into a nervous tic. It would be an awfully big one, if so. The world's biggest nervous tick. Like something a punch-drunk boxer might develop.

"M's a champion loser. A complete do-nothing."

"I think he's a winner," Amy said stoutly, remembering her vow to cherish and protect.

Laurie's face went into a spasm then went blank again.

Nailed her, Amy thought. Now I can be generous. "Laurie, let's be friends. We both love Masef . . ."

"No!" It was like a shout, only her voice was quiet and deadly. "I want him for my own. I've always wanted him. I've always loved him since I could first see. I can't live without him. He knows that. That's why he'll always come to see me. But he'll never stay for long. He'll never stay. Why does he stay with you?" She burst into harsh sobs. Like a man crying who didn't know how. It was awful. "Fuck," she said. "Oh, fuck!"

She shouldered by Amy who thought she was headed for the bathroom. She went instead to the bedroom, stood there looking wildly around. On her mirror Amy had stuck photos she'd taken of Masef. Laurie grabbed them. She looked in the closet as if to grab his clothes. Not finding any she slammed the door, bringing down a picture from the wall, the glass shattering. She looked at Amy's bed, covered in a summery floral comforter, as if she'd like to take a chain saw to it.

On her way out of the house, she knocked over a vase of purple and yellow irises—intentionally. More glass shattered, this time into a million shards because the vase was so fine. Steuben. It had been her mother's. Then she was gone. Feeling weak, Amy sat down. She'd been fairly okay while Laurie was there, but now she had to sit down, she felt so upset.

She had to sit down, she felt so scared.

SEVEN

The three years went by and it was time for me to establish myself as a world-class runner at the Boston Marathon.

With all my heart, I had wanted to go to Japan to train, but I could not afford it. Instead, I spent time in Eugene, Oregon, San Diego, California, and Salt Lake City, Utah with the best runners and coaches in America. While at Cal Berkeley, I ran with the track team.

I could run stride for stride with anyone in training runs, but it seemed I was not a good competitor because I never won any of the prominent races. It seemed, even after three years, that I was intimidated by the greatness of the runners I ran with, or else I so honored them that I could not bring myself to grind them into the dust, to bury them.

This was true at first. Then I stayed with this mindset and used it, as I thought, to my benefit.

Sometimes it seemed that in the home stretch, instead of pouring it on, I held back. The feeling among the other runners was that I had a mind problem and it was a shame.

They were right. I did. But it wasn't the mind problem they thought.

I ran four marathons during this three-year period.

The first three I purposely started ten minutes late, not going for the win but wanting only to examine my pacing and gain the experience.

The fourth was the Sacramento International Marathon where I qualified for Boston with an easy 2:18. This allowed me to be seeded in the first hundred at Boston so I could get off to a good start.

I was not sponsored like the other front runners, all of whom displayed their sponsor on their singlets and shorts. In fact, I broke precedent and didn't even wear a singlet, just yellow shorts and the old see-thru torso, my number pinned to the right leg of my shorts. What with that and my long blond wispy pigtail, and looking no more than sixteen, although I was now twenty-one, I didn't strike fear into anyone's heart, and to the runners who knew me I posed no threat.

That, of course, was the idea.

Still, my whippet-thin body, economy of motion, and seeming ability to keep both feet off the ground even while walking, gave one or two of the quality coursers pause.

It was April 17, a warm hazy morning in Hopkinton, Massachusetts. Five thousand runners, thirty of who were contenders. Just before the gun, men and women were doing warm-up sprints, slow jogs, or stretches.

Except for me. I stood quietly, trying to relax and center myself. I breathed deeply, completely emptying my lungs, then filling them up. I thought first of my mom and dad, hoping they were watching from wherever they were, motes of dust in the cosmic storm, then of Sister who I knew had her eyes pinned to the TV set, then of Ito, my true father, then of nothing except the words of Zen Master Tich Nhat

Han: "Breathing in I rest myself. Breathing out, I smile."

The gun.

I catapulted off with the front pack. It was the first time I had run with Japanese, Africans, and Europeans, although some of the Mexicans were familiar to me from California races. There were only three other Americans. I was surrounded by fabulous energy. It was fun. I was having fun. I smiled.

This was during the first fifteen miles which *are* fun because you feel so good, so fit, so ready you could bust out of your skin. Feeling giddy with strength and speed, you have to rein in and dole out the whole time to not give your race away to those seductive early miles.

The next five miles, fifteen to twenty, were serious running. Who's smiling now? Not me. This was serious, bordering on grim.

Then I entered the final six miles, which were a study in pain—a course I'd neglected to take.

I'd had no idea it would be this hard.

No idea because I had never duked it out before, preferring to hide my talent, save it for Boston, where I could astonish and amaze both runners and spectators by being the dark horse. From infancy, I'd always practiced secretly. When I vowed to be coached and join others, I still kept part of me secret, my speed, like a flame that had to be protected and nourished or it would go out. Or, crazily, it was as if I only had so much speed to spend and using it eventually would exhaust it.

Also, for Boston, I had wanted the advantage and mind-rest of nonentity.

Now I had to put the hammer down. Crush these guys. Or, more appropriately, blow them away.

The pack dwindled down and down. Runners fell back and away. Sometimes a runner pulled ahead and I had to decide whether to follow and show my hand, had to gauge carefully the worth of the other runners' display, which was often a last gasp attempt to take the lead before relinquishing it forever.

It was getting hard to stay with the front runners, let alone crush them. It was the hardest thing I'd ever done. These men were veterans. Pain was their brother. I began to doubt myself and to feel scared. They were leaving me now, incrementally pushing past the barrier of pain. I seemed unable to follow them. I didn't have it. I couldn't push past it and it didn't occur to me to leap over it. Negative thoughts poured down on me like rain. I didn't have it. I was a spoiled self-centered California kid and these were the great runners of the world.

I watched them go. First a foot or two of road opened between us, then yards. I watched the space grow as if the *road* was playing tricks on me, rather than my own failure to prevail.

Their energy field left with them. I was alone with the pain.

Then I remembered. Maybe pain is their brother, but speed is mine. This isn't only a contest of endurance, it's a race! My broken heart began to heal and to beat, to lighten up. My whole mind and body lightened and my psychic wings unfurled. This is what I'd been waiting for and working toward. This is why I was here. It was time to race!

I recaptured my place with the front four and when a fellow American runner pulled ahead, I went with him. The runner was unconcerned because he knew me and my "mind problem."

I went with him and then I left him. I wanted a

glorious finish, did not want to nip the noble runner at the last. So I surged. I pulled out all the stops and discovered that beyond the brutal, implacable pain was a place of no pain because when there is only a mile or so to go and you are winning, the pain takes a hike and the wings do the job. The smile returns. The body's at rest. I won in 2:06:43, a record for Boston and almost a world record.

It was at the finish line that I met Cecile. It was Cecile who put the winner's crown of laurel on my head.

"Why doesn't he have his hands up in the victory wave?" Masef asked. "Why isn't he smiling his head off and beating his chest the way winners do . . . and gorillas. Instead, he looks shell-shocked."

"He's been through a lot," said Masefield. "Something like a war. What an athlete. An amazing performance!"

Masef looked at his father, briefly wishing that he, as his son, could amaze him in this way. Or in any way. He knew he never would, which is why he only wished it briefly, like blowing out a match as soon as you light it.

"Yeah, but still . . ." Masef got back to his examination of Boy. "Everyone looks concerned. They probably are worried because he's so pale, not knowing that he's *always* that pale."

They were watching the tape of the marathon later the same day at Masefield's apartment in Washington, D.C.

"Everyone's saying who the hell *is* this guy anyhow? They probably think he's an alien. He looks like an alien and I don't mean a non-American, I mean an off-planetarian."

Masefield laughed,

Maybe I can't make him proud of me, but I always can make him laugh, Masef thought happily.

"His mother was a fantastic runner," Masefield remembered. "I *never* could beat her when we were kids. No one could. She'd race guys for money. I'd be her manager. Too bad there was no track for girls in those days."

"Boy always told me matter of factly that he was going to be the greatest runner in the world," Masef said, "and I'd think 'sure.'"

"Trueboy always speaks the truth."

"Look at that woman, Dad! Now the man's smiling. He might even be blushing. She's gorgeous."

Masefield looked at the woman crowning Boy. She looked ordinary to him. She looked like a small-town beauty queen, only older and thinner. But then, only one woman ever looked beautiful to him—Masef's mother.

"Speaking of gorgeous women," Masefield said while the tape was rewinding, cracking them both a beer, "Amy called. Very upset with me."

Masef ejected the tape, stood up and stretched, knocking his knuckles against the ceiling. "Upset with you, Dad? She *adores* you."

"I told Laurie about the two of you. Laurie searched her out and came by and smashed up the place literally and figuratively."

Masef sat down again. "Poor Laurie." He looked haggard.

"What about poor Amy?"

"Poor me when I go back home. Why did you tell Laurie?"

"She asked if you and Amy were lovers and I decided telling her might set her free."

"Nothing's going to set her free," Masef said glumly.

"I thought she might stop hoping and get on with her life."

"The killer for her would be that she always believed I didn't love her because I couldn't love any woman. That way, she could say to herself that if she couldn't have me, no other woman could either."

"Do you love Amy?"

"Not like I love Laurie. Or you. But I'm happy with her . . . happier than I've ever been, I guess. Why don't I love her, Dad? I just feel like she's not the one."

Masefield wished she was—even though they were cousins. Amy was a good girl. "Give yourself time. I never loved anyone before or since your mother. I was your age when I met her. Actually," he smiled, "I fell in love with her picture."

They had supper in, Masef cooking, regaling his father with tales of his recent travels, making him laugh. After supper Masefield went to his desk.

A couple of hours later, he took a break, strolled through the ample rooms in search of his son, his beloved but somehow hopeless son, thinking, he's still such a boy. He doesn't want to return to college and he doesn't want to work at anything.

Over the years he'd arranged jobs for him, but he never stayed with them, never got interested.

He poured himself some juice from a jar in the fridge, thinking, some young people don't know what they want to do. M knows—that he doesn't want to do anything—and seems perfectly content with the knowledge.

Why doesn't he grow up? Something to do with the

death of Buster was his mother's feeling. Also Laurie's belief.

He found M in front of the TV. He'd rolled forward the marathon tape, stopped it, and was staring at the woman crowning Boy. He sat down next to him on the couch. Masef threw an arm around his shoulder and kissed him on the cheek. The boy was so sweet. "What are your plans?" he asked him.

"Home to Amy by way of Inverness. I'll try to break my Washington to Inverness motorcycling record, which is how slow can I go without stopping anywhere more than a day. The key is to make endless stops, but none of them prolonged. Want to come?"

"It sounds like hell on earth."

"Okay, we'll go fast. We'll only stop for gas, meals, sunbathing, and movies."

"Actually," Masefield sighed slightly, "I meant what are your long-range plans?"

"I'll grow old and die," he said. "It's very sad."

"Yes," said his father, "it's a terrible arrangement."

In California, Sister watched the marathon live with friends. The whole time tears were in her eyes or coursing down her face.

Ito watched it at a friend's house in Stinson Beach, out on a deck, the sun-spangled Pacific Ocean gleaming behind the bleached-out screen. He, too, was moved and tears stood out in his eyes for, uncannily close though Sister was to Boy, Ito understood him better. He understood the shell-shocked look on his face at the end.

He did not run with *mushin,* Ito thought, the mind

that is without calculation or pretense, without contrivance.

Ito thought, knowing he ran without *mushin,* he can not love his win. Despite his tremendous accomplishment, he somehow feels his win was a trick. Too bad.

"Next time, Trueboy."

He tried to send him the thought that there would be another race he would win purely, but he felt a darkness, as if there would not be another race, would not be a "next time." Ito saw this darkness on the screen that was in front of the glimmering sea as Boy was being honored with the wreath of laurel.

Maybe it's a trick of the light, he thought. *If not, I'm seeing with the Dharma eye. I hope like hell it's a trick of the light.*

EIGHT

"Oh no!" Amy heard a car door slam, looked out the window and saw Laurie getting out of—a truck, of course. Amy was surprised she didn't drive a tank. Or a backhoe.

It was a warm, clear day in May, a month after the Boston Marathon. A visiting virtuoso mockingbird was singing from high in a Redwood.

She wasn't letting the woman in. No, sir. And she wasn't going out either. As far as Laurie was concerned, Amy was not home. She locked the door.

But Laurie didn't come to the door, instead shouted, "Hey Amy, heard you were moving. I'm going to the dump. Thought you'd have some stuff for me to take. Want to come?"

This was a very friendly shout. And Amy did have stuff for the dump, six bags full.

Also, although she'd stoutly told Laurie she'd learn about Masef from his own mouth, thank you very much, she was beginning to think she wouldn't and might as well hear it from Laurie's.

His life, as far as she knew so far, consisted of this. He'd spent his childhood in Inverness with his mother, visited often by Masefield. (His parents weren't separated—they just didn't live together because of Masefield's work.) At age twelve, he went to

Andover, a New England boarding school, spending vacations with his father in D.C. He went to U.C. Santa Cruz for two years then dropped out. Since then, as she saw with her own eyes, he had held various jobs about which he was indifferent, among them taking over Boy's cooking stint at the Cactus Cafe.

He had lots of friends. He was a dear lover, a good-natured, thoughtful roommate.

Except that he had dropped out of college, to which he might one day return, what was there in all this that would constitute his being a "loser?"

She did not believe for one minute that he travelled to "get away from her," as Laurie had said, but she had come to believe and accept that when he left her he went to see Laurie and she didn't like the feeling she got when she thought about it.

Laurie told her that he came but he didn't "stay." Did she mean he didn't stay forever in the way that Laurie wished he would, that he stayed for a short while, or that he only dropped in briefly, just to say goodbye? How long exactly did he stay with Laurie . . . the woman he'd "loved all his life?" This was one thing she might learn from Laurie on their travel to the dump.

She was not going to descend to jealous feelings and become a pitiful maniac like Laurie. But she wasn't going to be ill-treated either. She wanted to know what was what. She wanted Masef to be straight with her. If he wasn't, then he *was* a loser. If she wasn't woman enough for Masef, then he wasn't man enough for her.

So Amy stepped out of the house, but she definitely pulled the door shut behind her, thereby preserving what remained of the pictures and vases.

"Hi, Laurie. How'd you know I was moving?"

"Talked to Masefield. He always knows every-thing."

She was dressed in jeans and a grey sweatshirt with the arms cut off—a muscle shirt. No makeup. Nor did she need it. Never would with that perfect skin, chis-eled features, fabulous teeth. Although makeup might be worth it if it could cover up the meanness, Amy thought.

Amy wore baggy khaki shorts and a pink T-shirt. Her hair was in a French braid. "Has Masef been by to see you?" she asked. She hadn't seen him since before Laurie's last visit, although he'd called from his father's apartment in Washington a few days after the marathon.

"No. We've just talked by phone."

Amy led the way to her trash pile and Laurie fol-lowed. They each took two of the bulging green plastic bags to the truck; Amy dragging, Laurie carry-ing. "He's in Inverness now," Laurie said, tossing the bags into the truck bed on top of her load of brush. "He comes to see me before he goes on a trip, but always goes home to Inverness first thing when he gets back." Laurie went for the last two bags, Amy following empty-handed.

"To see his Mom?" Amy asked. It was natural to go to see his Mom before her, she thought fairly. After all, they weren't married, she and Masef. Why shouldn't he go home to Inverness first?

"Mainly to see Buster. Tell him all about what he's been doing. Only Buster gets to know, really."

Buster? Amy wondered. Who the hell was Buster? She wasn't going to ask and show her ignorance. Not yet anyhow. "Oh," she responded. She remembered that had been her predominant response on the occa-sion of Laurie's last visit. She wished she'd stayed hidden in the house and not gotten involved in the bag-dragging. The entire conversation so far had been forced and fake—on her side anyhow.

"Amy, I'm sorry about last time," Laurie surprised her by saying. "You said let's be friends. I'd like to be." As Laurie spoke, she threw a tarp over the load and began roping it down with intricate knots.

Amy couldn't see any reason to be friends at this point. "What changed your mind?" she asked suspiciously.

"I'll be honest with you. It's because I don't think M loves you. You don't feel like a threat to me anymore."

Amy felt stabbed in the heart. This was a friend she could do without. She determined not to say oh. "He loves you more, I suppose?"

Laurie seemed to consider. "I don't know about more. But I'm pretty sure about always." She laughed harshly. "Don't worry. You still get to sleep with him, not me."

Well, that was one question answered. She was Masef's only lover. That was the main thing, wasn't it? Anyhow, why believe Laurie about anything?

"Come on." Laurie got in the cab.

Amy didn't want to go, wished she could retrieve her trash and cut the connection. But it was all tarped over and tied down now. She was committed to the journey. Trapped would be a better word.

She got in and pretty soon, as they took the freeway exit toward San Quentin prison and the nearby waste-disposal site, she gave in to gnawing curiosity and resignedly asked, "Who's Buster?"

"Buster's a grave."

Amy didn't say oh. She waited.

"You know Masefield's Ecclesiastes quote that he

likes so much about living life with all your might because there ain't nothing for you in the grave, man, nothing to do in the grave where you go?"

"Yes. I know it." Now they turned off the prison road passing the Marin Rod and Gun club. For all her years in the county, this was her first trip to the dump, a foreign territory. And since she'd been working for the local paper, she'd hardly left town for months. She felt, having gone ten miles away, as if she were on a journey.

Why do I stay home so much? she asked herself. *Is it because I'm always waiting for Masef? Is that what I am? A waiter. Am I working at home so I don't have to leave home? It's pathetic.*

How long ago it seems, that day when Masefield told me the quote. I was in the passage (the hole), hideously depressed, floundering. Now I have work I love, a man I love. At least that's what I thought up until a minute ago. When I began to feel like some sort of shut-in, waiting for a man who goes to see Buster before he comes home to me. Buster, who I never even heard of, *is the preferred one.*

"A grave?"

"Yeah, M isn't waiting to go to his own grave," Laurie said. "He goes to Buster's. He loved Buster so much. Buster was his real father, as far as he was concerned, and Masefield his biological one."

Like Boy feels about Ito, Amy thought.

"Life just stopped for him when Buster died. He was only four years old, almost five. Or at least life *mattering* stopped." They were entering the disposal site now, Laurie braking at the booth, forking over twenty dollars, the sum for which the woman in the booth gauged the load to be worth—not the price of the load, really, Amy thought, but the price of the emptiness which the truck would contain when they

left. Amy tried to contribute money but Laurie fanned
her off.

"Both of our folks died and life didn't stop for us,"
Amy commented, picking up the thread of their talk,
feeling Laurie's explanation was too slick. "And we
were teenagers."

Laurie adeptly backed the truck to the edge of the
gorge and cut the engine.

"Maybe that's why. You already had a handle on
life when you lost your folks. But M lost Buster and
just before that another terrible thing happened,
which was that he was lost at sea for over twenty-four
hours and no one knew what happened with him during that lost time. All he said afterward was that his
grandmother saved him, Sunny's mom. Only thing
was—her mom had been dead for five years."

"God!"

They dropped the conversation while they worked
together to free the load and toss it over into the
gorge where the bulldozers roamed, pushing the
dumped trash around in a seemingly random fashion.
Amy considered all that was needed was fire for it to
be a vision of hell. It made her feel nauseous to look
down at all the mauled detritus of life on earth being
pushed endlessly to and fro. A tiny, fragile blue butterfly floated by like a lost angel.

Laurie flung off her load of refuse with zest, then
swept the truck bed clean while Amy folded the tarp
and coiled the rope and examined her ruined nails.

Laurie reached into a Styrofoam cooler for a beer,
cracked it open and guzzled it down, surveying the
landscape with pleasure—as if it were Versailles, Amy
thought. What a strange woman.

"I love dumps," she said. "This hauling business
put me through college, but now I just want to keep

on hauling. I'm my own boss, work in my own sweet time, and make thirty thousand a year."

Also, you get to drink on the job, Amy added silently. *Drink and brag.*

Back on the road, Amy resumed their talk, no longer trying to disguise or protect her pitiful ignorance regarding her lover she'd lived with the last three years, sensing a tragedy that put such feelings of embarrassment in the shade. She remembered Masef saying of his mother, "A man died because of her." Was that Buster?

She asked Laurie, "How did Buster die?"

"It's a long story and you really should hear it from M," Laurie said, having maddeningly taken Amy's line for her own. "It's called, The Legend of Buster."

Oh great, thought Amy. *Just when I cave in and practically beg, she clams up.*

Laurie creased her brow and added, with obvious difficulty, "The bullet came out of Bart's gun and at the same time Masefield killed Bart."

Bart? Amy wondered. Another strange, unheard name out of her lover's life. What did she and Masef talk about?

"Bart was my grandfather."

"Masefield killed your grandfather!" This was getting unbelievably farfetched. Lost at sea. Murderers. Ghosts. Give me a break. Generational assassinations? Could Laurie be putting her on? Or be a compulsive liar?

"Yes. He had to kill him. It wasn't the first time Masefield killed someone because he had to. Or the last. He believes there are times when one has to kill, when it's right to do so. He calls it the exception."

Amy wondered how many times you killed before

it stopped being an exception. *It seems like there should be a cut-off number,* she thought.

Laurie looked at Amy, saying with complete sincerity, "I could kill if I had to."

She seemed to want a response from Amy. "Oh" certainly wouldn't do the job. Have you considered therapy? seemed tame.

Then, unbelievably, Laurie said, "In fact, it crossed my mind I could push you off into the dump, just as the bulldozer was coming along to turn you under all that shit and bury you. It would look like an accident."

Amy was chilled. The woman was dead serious. She managed to ask in a small voice, "Why didn't you?"

"I decided I didn't have to. It wouldn't be right. It wasn't an exception."

NINE

Luckily, Laurie left Amy off at the bottom of the driveway because when she got to the house, Masef was in the yard, lying on the lounge. He leapt up and came to meet her. "Where've you been?" he asked as if it were Amy, not he, who had been gone two months.

He looked tanned and fit and happy, which is how he always looked.

"Actually I've just been to the dump with your pal, Laurie."

"Oh, yeah?" He looked pleased.

"Yes. She heard I was moving and thought I might have some stuff to take."

"How sweet. That's just like Laurie."

Amy didn't disenchant him, didn't tell him she was so sweet that her real reason had been to dispose of her at the disposal site, except the bulldozer just never seemed to be passing by at the right minute for her to pull off the job. Nor did she tell him that he loved her so little, according to Laurie, it didn't matter anyhow whether she lived or died, being no kind of threat.

By now they were next to each other and Masef was standing with his arms out to embrace her, but she was almost cringing away. She really wanted to hug him and be hugged. She'd missed him so much. She was starved for love and affection. But she sure wasn't going to throw herself into his arms if he didn't love her. Or if he really thought Laurie was "sweet."

Masef didn't notice her dilemma and swept her into his arms, covering her face with kisses. "You look beautiful. I'm so happy to be home. If there is a home. What do you mean you're moving?"

"Just to the little cottage."

"Me, too?"

"Well . . ." She didn't look at him, ". . . if you want?"

"What do you mean? Of course, I want. Aren't we a couple?"

"Are we?"

"Are you mad at me that I went away this time? Why was this time different? What's wrong?"

"Oh, Masef. Laurie's been telling me all these things. She says you don't love me. She told me about this guy, Buster, you loved so much and who *you never even mentioned* to me in all the years we've been to-gether. Is that being a couple?"

He released her from his embrace, stepping away. The mockingbird began singing its head off, as if this were a moment to celebrate. "There's nothing to say about Buster, that's why. I was only *four years old!* I don't even remember him."

"She said you go to his grave."

"It's just a place to go where I feel good. I like to plant a few things, keep it looking nice." He swal-lowed. "Buster loved flowers."

He looked at Amy who seemed to be waiting for more. "I told him about my motorcycle trip. He used to race them. That was before I was born, but then he stopped because he knew it was dangerous and that Sunny and I needed him." He scowled, realizing he was rambling. "Laurie's always going on about me and Buster. She thinks I'm some kind of cripple because he died when I was young. Look at you, for God's sake. You lost *both* parents."

"I know." Amy wondered if she was, deep down, a cripple because of it. Probably.

"Will you tell me the legend of Buster?" Amy softly pleaded, not wanting to know the story so much as wanting Masef to include her, wanting to be a part of him in the place that it mattered.

Masef glowered. "No, I won't." He walked up and down holding his arms a funny way. When he turned, Amy saw that both his hands were pressed against his heart, one hand on the other, as if stanching blood. Amy's hands flew to her own heart, feeling frightened for him. She could tell he didn't know what he was doing.

"Masefield tells that story," he said. "He keeps the legend alive like it was a sacred duty." Masef laughed, now flinging his arms wide, shrugging, shrugging the whole thing off as unimportant.

Amy's arms dropped to her sides, slightly reached toward him.

"I knew Buster when I was little. I was just a baby, a toddler, and he was just a local guy who loved Sunny and me. He looked after us while Masefield was in prison. He was—he was good as gold."

Just then Masef started to cry. His face crumpled and tears ran down. He began to choke. "He was so good, Buster was."

What have I done? Amy thought. *What a bitch I am. Laurie should have killed me.*

"Oh Masef. I'm sorry." Amy wanted to take him

and rock him in her arms, but he was a hard man to get her arms around, let alone hold and rock—he was so rangey, so gangly. She wrapped her arms around his waist and looked up at him. "I love you Masef. I love you with all my heart. I'm so glad you're back."

Why hadn't she greeted him this way to begin with? Why? Why?

He threw his head back to look at the sky so she couldn't see his face. He heaved a huge, wracking sigh. Then he looked down, smiled, joked.

"I was just crying because you won't let me live with you in the little cottage. That's why."

"Of course, I will. I never said I wouldn't. How could I live without you?"

"You probably think I'll take up all the room."

"That's true." Amy recovered, moved into his joking mode. "Yes, that's very true. Maybe we could add a wing for your legs."

He laughed. He picked her up in his arms and swung her around. "Two wings. One for each leg. And we should add on a place for Boy's wings, a hall of fame for his wings. But, wait a minute, *why* are you moving in there. What about Boy?"

"Boy's moving into the big house. With his wings and his soon-to-be wife. And her baby."

TEN

I was a hero when I met Cecile. Illuminated by fame and flashbulbs, surrounded by cheering crowds, I appeared glamourous despite the fact that, ugly to begin with, I was looking my worst—wasted, even withered from the effort and, as Masef told me later, shell-shocked, not to mention so pale you couldn't just see through to my organs but through to what I was standing in front of.

Just as an ill man falls in love with the nurse who puts a cool hand on his brow, an exhausted hero loves the woman who crowns him. She looked so cool, so perfect, every hair in place—she symbolized effort-lessness at a time when I'd majored in effort. All she ever had to do, I thought, was stand there and be pretty. I was dazzled. She gave my salt-streaked face a kiss, my mouth too, and not a peck, a real kiss. Luckily, I'd had water by then and my glue-like saliva was dissolved.

I grabbed her hand. "Don't leave me." I wanted more kisses, and only from her. Forever.

She gave me this long, serious look as if it were a major decision. "I'll be waiting for you," she gestured around, "when you're through with all this."

After that, we only parted company when I was off on a run or an interview. I stayed around New England for over a month, being feted by all and sundry, being swamped with money, being loved by Cecile.

"I'm in love," I told Sister, calling her daily. "And she loves me! It's unbelievable. She wouldn't have looked twice at me if we'd met elsewhere. What a lucky break that I happened to be the winner. Just wait until you meet her."

She was a fairy princess. That's what her father called her, "Princess." She was small and voluptuous with blond curly hair, big blue eyes. Perhaps her mouth was a little narrow for the size of her eyes and her chin receded a bit, like mine. If I looked like a bird, she resembled a rabbit, and she burrowed while I soared, preferring to lie around indoors most of the day to being out and about. She was as warm and cuddly as my bony beaky body was not. It was like a cross-species mating, but it worked. My orgasms turned my body inside out and she said she'd never been penetrated by such energy. Like being electrocuted, she said. Strange analogy, granted, but the French call climax the little death and ours was a big one—hers by charge and mine by reversible anatomy.

Her father, Mike Rodd, was a local politician, which was how she came to be the "crowner," and he was a man who, attractive in his youth, still retained that image of himself, and carried himself accordingly, although he had, in fact, become repellent looking—corpulent and hard-faced. The mother, as is often the case with the wives of such men, was a fool. She was pretty to look at, and endlessly pleasant, but her conversation was on a grade-school level, without the charm that sometimes attends a kid talking.

I hasten to say that Cecile was college educated, smart and articulate.

Then there was Baby. Of course, I loved it that

Cecile called her "Baby." Equally impressive was the fact that she had a cat called "Puss."

"Call me Girl," she said laughing. "Then we can be Boy, Girl, Baby, and Puss—a storybook family."

"Not storybook so much as first reader. And Girl is a pretty big comedown from Princess. In fact, it's demeaning."

"Then so is Boy."

"I have a feeling I'll never shake Boy. I'll be Boy at fifty. How embarrassing."

All this literalism of mine that had so ordered my youth began to seem childish. I vowed to do better about calling Sister Amy.

"You're Boy to all the world now," Cecile said. "No good changing your name just when you're famous."

"Tell it to Mohammed Ali and Abdul Jabar."

She understood my feelings about Freeling and was anxious to take the name for her own (Although the freeling business began to seem stupid to me, too. Maybe you simply don't need handles when you're in love and a champion.) We only delayed because I wanted to be married at home with Amy there, and Ito. Luckily, Cecile didn't want to be married in New England because that's where her first marriage had been.

"She's a widow," I told Amy. "And she's got a little baby around two years old. She was pregnant when her husband died. Isn't that sad? It helps that we've both lost family. It adds another dimension. Everyone seems to treat her with a sort of reverence because of her loss, making me feel like I'm taking away a priceless treasure which I've got to guard with my life. No problem. That's how I feel, too. Of course, I've told her all about you. And Masef. Oh, boy, Amy, our family is getting so big!"

Poor Amy, all these calls where she couldn't get a word in. I was euphoric. To have had a major dream realized, and then on top of that fall in love and be loved in return, not to mention the money and recognition! Euphoria is too mild a word.

Our homecoming was wonderful. Amy had cleaned the house so that it shone like new. There were flowers on every surface, a spread of food, bottles of champagne in coolers. Friends were gathered to celebrate, about thirty people. There were banners, live music. It was great. The happiest day of my life.

I hadn't even asked Amy if we could live in the house and there she had it all ready for us. She'd even fixed up a nursery room for Baby. The most touching thing was that, unable to successfully remove my quotes from the cottage wall to have them in the house, Masef removed the wall itself, cut out the plasterboard, and set it up in my new bedroom. Since the wall was down anyhow, Masef was going to extend the little cottage to make it bigger—"a wing for his legs," said Amy.

I hung my laurel wreath on the wall of quotes.

They had also given me the gift of new quotes. This from Roger Bannister, who was the first to break the four-minute mile: "Running brings a joy, a freedom, a challenge, not found anywhere." Love does too! I'm here to tell you!

And Peter Snell's great understatement regarding his double Golds at the Tokyo Olympics for the eight- and fifteen-hundred meters, "It was a nice sort of feeling."

What did I feel about my Boston? It's so hard to break free of habitual responses to anything, but maybe especially to winning. Most of the gestures and comments winners make are copied from other athletes down through the years, even though a man would not be a champion were he not an especially individual, original person. It's just easier to use given words rather than tap into your own true feelings which, if you did discover at the source, you might be wary of vocalizing.

When you're wearing a wreath and everyone's cheering and they put a mike up to your lips, you don't want to say, "I feel awful. I'm tired. I'm scared. I could have run faster. I should have done it differently. Leave me alone."

When you have worked so hard for so long and thought of nothing else, you know you're supposed to feel happy, accomplished, triumphant, so you act that way to not confuse people's expectations.

I did feel happy at my homecoming. It was a nice sort of feeling.

Everyone was enchanted with Cecile and Amy embraced her as a sister, even though she refused the hand wrestle initiation, seeing ahead to the inevitable dunking. Masef, too, thought she was wonderful and pulled from all his store of humor and antics to please her. Later, he wooed her out onto the boardwalk to hand wrestle and at the first slight twitch of her little hand he threw himself into the pond.

Ito was away and didn't get to meet her then. The only one with whom she didn't seem to hit it off was Masefield.

ELEVEN

"What do we know about Cecile?" Masefield asked
Amy a few weeks after the welcome-home party.
They were alone together in the little cottage, which
Amy had made charming in a way Boy never did. Just
removing the weights and bench press added a lot of
charm. As usual, she had vases of flowers (Masef
loved flowers, too, and bought exotic bouquets, as
well as putting seeds in the ground that came up like
magic). There was a Futon with a quilt she had made
herself, a few sticks of furniture she'd painted in pastel washes. Her own black-and-white photographs
were scattered on the white walls.

Masef's contribution, besides flowers, was the hole
in the wall, still unextended. Luckily, it wasn't the
rainy season. His guitar and back-pack were in one
corner, lending an air of poetic impermanence to the
encampment. There was also a long, slim leather case
that could have contained a wind instrument or a pool
cue, but which Masefield knew was his son's cher-
ished fishing pole.

"Oh, Masefield," Amy teased him. "You always
have to *know*. The royal investigator."

The others were in the big house watching a movie
when Masefield appeared at her door, a finger to his
lips so she wouldn't scream out an excited greeting as

she always did. He wanted to keep his presence quiet to allow for a confidential talk.

Amy told Masefield what she knew about Cecile, stressing the main thing, which was how happy her brother was, how much in love. But Masefield wasn't interested in the main thing.

"How did her husband die?" he asked.

He sprawled loosely in a chair, smoking by the open window to not defile Amy's environment. She'd poured him a glass of Corvoisier, which she kept on hand especially for him knowing he was partial to it, although Masef declared himself jealous.

("Am I to drink California brandy, then, while he gets the French?" "Oh, Masef, you don't even drink cognac, you're a beer drinker." "That's just because I can't pronounce cognac.")

Amy, trying to remember how Cecile's husband died, responded, "I'm not sure, Masefield. I think it was a hunting accident."

"Oh?" Masefield raised his brows. "The old hunting accident story, eh?"

Amy laughed. "Well, that's better than the old gun-cleaning story." Then she blushed. "You know, it might actually have been a gun-cleaning accident. Anyhow, he was a hunter . . . I think." Amy threw up her hands. "I'm confused. I'm sure Boy told me, but I just don't remember. Apparently, it's extremely painful for her to talk about."

"I bet." His violet eyes were distant, thoughtful, physically like Masef's, but utterly dissimilar in their expressions. He puffed, sipped, adjusted his sprawl by crossing his ankles.

"What's troubling you?" Amy asked.

"She's cute all right, sexy for sure. She's vivacious, although lacking in humor, which is the next thing to lacking in soul. Maybe the same thing," he decided, dismissing most of the world if so, relegating it to subhumanism. "I guess I've always distrusted women who wear a lot of makeup."

Amy frowned. Amy wore makeup.

"They put on a face and don't let you see behind it."

Amy still frowned.

"Okay, forget the makeup. Her eyes are not the windows of her soul. They're mirrors she can see out of but other people can't see into. Instead, they get exaggerated reflections of themselves that she sends back to flatter them."

Amy tried to envision Cecile's eyes. They were bright and happy. Unlike her own, which always had shadows under them—despite makeup.

"When she speaks, she doesn't engage. It's not a conversation—it's a show. It strikes me that she's wholly self-centered."

"People adore her. They sit at her feet!" Amy protested.

"Because they can't sit beside her, can't be intimate."

"Boy says she's very loving."

"He has no one with whom to compare her. No one ever loved him but you."

"Ito loves him."

"Ito loves everyone, all sentient beings."

"But Ito loves Boy like a son."

"No, he doesn't love in given ways. He's beyond that."

"Poor Ito."

Masefield smiled.

Amy swallowed cognac. This was all pretty depress-

ing. She did not like to think her hero could be
wrong, but she believed that he was.

What if he were right? What did that mean for
Boy?"

"Has Ito met her?" Masefield asked.

"No. He's away."

"Ito will know."

Amy wondered *what* Ito would know.

"When are they going to get married?"

"Not for another month."

"That's good. There's time."

They were silent. Then: "What about me and
Masef?" she asked Masefield. "I feel like Laurie's
completely poisoning our relationship now that she
knows about it."

"Laurie's a good person. She wouldn't do anything
to harm Masef's happiness and she knows he's happy
with you."

"Good person? Are you kidding? Masefield, I'm
beginning to think you don't understand women at
all!"

Amy saw glass splintering. Bulldozers.

His saying that about Laurie completely discredited
his assessment of Cecile as far as Amy was concerned.

"Laurie acts out and she's got a big mouth, but her
heart is in the right place."

Amy shook her head. She said awkwardly, painfully, "The last couple of weeks Masef hasn't wanted
to make love to me." God, it felt good to tell someone. She felt like she'd pulled a plug and her heart's
blood could start coursing again. "I know Laurie's
behind it, Masefield. I'm sure of it."

"Laurie's been on a hunting trip in Montana."

Maybe she'll have a hunting accident, Amy thought.

". . . so I know he hasn't seen her or talked to

her. Maybe you're poisoning the relationship because you *think* Laurie's come between you."

Masefield was right. It wasn't what Laurie said, it was what she herself did with it, how she let it effect her, that caused the harm. She hadn't even given Masef a warm welcome home, instead made him feel unwanted, interrogated him about Buster, made him cry. She should never have gone to the dump with her and let her twist her around.

"Laurie's always been there for Masef. She always will be. Just as Boy will be for you. You'll have to accept it."

She decided not to bring up Laurie's willingness to kill if she had to. If Laurie was right about Masefield being of the same philosophy, it would only increase his respect for her. He might not see the difference (as Laurie didn't seem to) between killing for reasons of jealousy and for reasons of national security. As for killing grandfathers . . .

"Masefield, will you tell me the legend of Buster?"

Masefield told her the legend but not the whole truth, which only he knew. He told a story of love, madness, murder, and greatness of soul. Amy understood why soul was important to Masefield from hearing this story of Buster: a foundling at age four, mute for another four years, who grew to a man of physical courage, intellectual invention, and loving heart. In high school he fell in love with Sunny Scott and loved her until the day he died at age twenty-four. Buster loved Masef like his own son because Sunny was the love of his life—even though Masefield was the great love of hers.

It was a haunting tale, a sad one. Amy cried. Masefield's voice shook in the telling, but he was not a person who cried. They were both a bit drunk at this point. It was the most wonderful evening Amy ever had.

She felt blessed with the richness of her family relationships, the goodness of her life. The trouble with Masef would pass, was already beginning to pass, now that she'd spoken of it. She'd been suffering unnecessarily. She only had to get her mind right about Laurie, then things would be well between Masef and herself.

It grew dark with the passing of time until moonlight began glistening on the leaves of a fig tree whose serpentine branches embraced the little cottage.

What with being so happy about this rare, long, solitary visit with Masefield, so moved by the legend, and partly relieved of her own trouble, she forgot his insidious doubts about Cecile. Anyhow, the story he told corroborated her earlier feeling that it was men Masefield understood, not women.

TWELVE

The next morning when Amy reached for Masef and he flinched away from her, all her suffering came back down on her like an avalanche of ice and snow. She remembered Masefield telling her, "Ito will know," saying it in such a way of utter certainty and trust, with what for Masefield amounted to minor reverence. It occurred to Amy that Ito might "know" what she should do about Laurie.

Although not as close to Ito as Boy, she knew him well enough to talk intimately with him. She had spent her college vacations at the Sacramento house where Boy had lived with him, their own house being rented out at the time.

It was essential to talk with someone who had not known Laurie since she was a child, and therefore was not blinded to what Amy believed to be her truly rotten nature.

She didn't want to bring her worries and fears to Boy at this time, which for him was so celebratory and happy.

Ito now lived in Stinson Beach, but was currently on a retreat with the Lama Tara Tulka Rimpoche, visiting from Tibet. (Actually India, thanks to the Chinese, Boy explained, who drove Tara Tulka and his holy ilk from their sacred land, burning their monasteries.). She knew it was an unconscionable act to disturb Ito at the monastery, but that's how desperate she felt after yet another week more of Masef turning from her in the night and flinching from her in the morning.

During the day, when she sometimes spontaneously hugged him, he returned it paternally, patting her on the back in the way that a parent does, as if to say, "there, there." It made her feel unlovely and diminished. She felt like a child or sister.

He hardly looked at her. It was as if she weren't there—or as if he wished she weren't. There was no warmth, affection, fun. He didn't tease her or play with her. No roughhousing. No touching at all.

What pain. She felt there were rocks in her heart. She was so tense her voice changed, as if there were a noose around her throat. Masef didn't notice. The noose kept her from eating, too. She pined.

He brought her no flowers, customarily an almost daily occurrence. Why bring flowers to a person you don't look at?

When she tried to broach the subject of his coldness to her, he frowned and grew silent. She didn't want to press it for fear he'd hoist his back-pack and guitar and be gone. He never had left to "get away from her"; she didn't want him to start now.

The day she decided to seek out Ito, she spent the morning developing photos in the darkroom that had once been a larder next to the laundry room. She came blinking into the sun to find her family—Masef, Boy, Cecile, Baby—all out on the front lawn. Cecile lay on a lounge. Masef raked grass left from his mowing. Boy was trying to teach Baby to crawl, but Baby wasn't having any of it. Boy crawled around the lawn in an exaggerated slow motion. Everyone laughed except Baby.

Amy didn't join them but went right to her car on the graveled driveway, a ten-year-old Alfa Romeo Spider that had been her mother's, the car Dad didn't crash; the car Mom took to her suicide, drove to the bridge, parked at Vista Point, left to walk a quarter of a mile out where, lithe and strong, she climbed over the high railing.

Maybe she stood on the iron lip for a while before jumping, gazing at the sky, or the city, or down at the water that looked strangely inviting. Maybe the same motion that took her over the railing carried her without pause on her launch into space, onward as if sailing out and over—but only for a split second—because then it was downward. Rocketing, plummeting, to bone-breaking, organ-crushing death.

Amy had learned that ninety miles an hour is the speed at which a human body falls.

They found her broken body the next day, and the note she left in the car for her children. "I'm sorry, my darlings, but I can't live without your father. The pain is insupportable. Take care of each other. We love you."

Sure.

Boy always parked the Volvo inside the garage, Amy her Alfa out. Last night, because she'd left the top down, a spider had spun a web connecting the wheel and the dash. Sadly, it had to be wrecked, although she preserved the spider. Amy could relate to homemaking, it being her own forte in life.

She backed down the driveway shouting, "Okay," to Boy's cry of "Toilet paper!" and Masef's of *"New York Times!"* for they assumed this was the normal mundane run to town, not a holy pilgrimage.

How many people in America, Any wondered, get to drive a twisting mountain road and, in less then half an hour from their home, enter the tranquil beauty of a Zen Buddhist monastery set in a narrow, green gorge between high golden hills next to the deep blue sea?

She parked at the beach and walked back a mile or so along the hillside trail, then on through the Zen center's vegetable and flower gardens, which seemed confined and subdued compared to the wildflowers which glinted on the attendant hills—like smithereens from a celestial accident.

The community was leaving the dining room as Amy approached the cluster of wooden buildings— about thirty people, some with shaved heads, all dressed in the customary dark clothes, some in black robes.

Amy did not see the big Samoan in their number.

She heard laughter from within. Cautiously, she peeped into the dining room and saw a few men talking together. Tara Tulka, enfolded in a red toga-like garment was speaking in Tibetan, his face alight with what Amy perceived to be not holiness so much as *joie de vivre.* The faces around him reflected this joy, their eyes sparkling. The language sounded more European than Asian to Amy. His gestures were elegant, arms and hands moving as if in dance.

The translator, a big rough-hewn man in jeans and plaid shirt, seemed to inhale Tara's words, then exhale them in American lingo. The two were in tune, speaking as one man.

The third man, features chiseled and contained, was the abbott of the monastery, sitting motionlessly in an arranged robe of black and brown. The fourth, Ito, in black jeans and T-shirt, did not, as was usual

with him, fill the room with his force. He had somehow tamped down his energy field in honor of their
guest. Or else the Lama, by virtue of his kindly, joy-
ous nature, had banked the fires of the holy warrior.

Amy did not intrude, but found a seat in the court-
yard to await her friend.

Who came at once. "Amy, I saw you looking in. Is
Boy in trouble?"

"No, Ito, Boy is ecstatically happy but I . . ."

Amy felt ashamed of her small, selfish problem. It
did not loom large in this place. It was no bigger than
one of the poppies on the huge presiding hills, this
small problem, embarrassingly sexual in nature, for
that's what it amounted to really; she'd floundered
into this profound place to whine to Ito that Masef
wouldn't bed her.

"Come along." He led her to a bench overlooking
a small marshy pond or wet place. "Tell me." The
bright slivers of his eyes were kindly and encourag-
ing.

She told. About Laurie's first visit to the house—
how aggrieved, resentful, jealous and violent she was
—and the second visit, the dump trip. "She said she
had considered killing me, but figured she didn't really need to since Masef loved her more than me at
this point. Not that she couldn't change her mind at a
moment's notice. She's probably waiting for the day."

"You have been blessed with an enemy, Amy."

"Blessed?" Amy's heart sank. Ito's response was, if
anything, worse than Masefield's had been during
their talk in the cottage.

"What an opportunity for you to practice patience
and tolerance. In fact, having an enemy is the neces-
sary condition for this practice."

"Practice patience! Give me a break, Ito. This woman wants to bury me in garbage!"

Ito ignored her, sounding his own plaint. "Surrounded by beloved friends as I am, it's *easy* to be good, to think of them before myself. It is a pleasure. Now, if I only had a good enemy to contend with, to really prove my mettle as a compassionate person, then I'd be in business. I'd be on my way."

He looked at her jealously.

"But Ito . . ."

"This woman really hates you."

"Yes! Yes, she does, Ito! And meanwhile, Masef turns from me. And won't even talk to me about it. Won't talk to me or look at me. He won't make love to me, Ito, hasn't for weeks!"

"That's where the patience comes in. Let him be. He'll speak when he's able. He'll embrace you when he's able. These things can't be forced. The boy's in some sort of trouble that may have nothing to do with Laurie."

"I know it does," Amy said crankily.

Ito smiled patiently. Lacking an enemy, he at least had a crank.

"You must be on the alert with this woman but also practice tolerance, just as you have done already when she's acted out so viciously."

"That wasn't tolerance I was practicing; it was terror."

Ito laughed. "Well maybe it looked like tolerance to her. And maybe she was grateful. Or at least confounded. Anyhow, don't put yourself in striking distance. No more trips to the dump. And keep her out of your house. But most of all, don't play into her hands by trying to cling to Masef. What he loves about you is that you let him be. That you let him come and go and glory in him for the man that he is, even though he is nothing. Laurie will always try to make something of him to her own standards. She is a strong woman. But you can be stronger. By being kinder."

"So, what you're really saying is, do nothing."

"Right. But do nothing alertly." He stood up, blocking out the landscape, dwarfing the hills. The ocean was a wet place now, the pond only a tear.

"Okay. I'll try. Thanks Ito." Amy stood up, kissed his cheek, and walked away.

"Patience makes us beautiful," he called after her. "Already your beauty is enhanced."

"But does it make us sexy?" she responded ringingly, then was horribly abashed to see a file of monks turn her way.

"You know that sex is not an issue," he shouted over the heads of the unastonished monks. "It only seems like it is. Don't let it sidetrack you." He waved and turned back toward the Zendo.

Feeling better, feeling really well, Amy returned home, not forgetting toilet paper and *The New York Times.*

THIRTEEN

Normally, Amy would have talked to me, not Ito. This was the first time in our lives she didn't come to me with her trouble. But she didn't want to disturb what she perceived to be my "happy celebratory time."

That time, sorrowfully, did not last much beyond the welcome-home party. When she told Ito, I was ecstatically happy, she was far off the mark. When he asked her, "Is Boy in trouble?" he was right to be concerned. I was in trouble, big trouble, and Ito, as usual, "knew."

Amy was too deep in her own problem to wonder at Ito asking about me, or she would have come to me and we could have put our two troubles together.

It wasn't long after we were home and settled in that Cecile and I had two serious fights.

The first one was because, while rummaging in her bureau for a shawl she'd sent me for, I found a gun.

I ran to the living room. "Cecile. I found a gun. Is it yours?"

She was lying on the couch reading *Vogue.*

"Yes." She continued to flip the pages.

"Why?"

Hearing the strain in my voice, she sat up, putting aside the magazine.

"I've always had a gun. Daddy taught me to shoot when I was a teenager. A woman alone needs a gun."

"But Cecile, you're not alone now. You're with me."

"Darling, of course, I am. But," she laughed, "although you're the world's fastest runner, you're not exactly a brute of a man."

I sat down next to her, putting my arms around her. "This is a safe little town. We hardly need to lock the doors. You don't need to worry. Let's get rid of it. I don't want a gun in our home."

Up to then, she'd been acting cute and affectionate as always, touching and kissing as she talked. Now, she drew away and frowned. "No."

"Didn't your husband die from a gunshot?" I asked, cursing the tremble in my voice.

"Yes," she answered neutrally.

"I should think you'd loathe the very idea of the thing being around."

"It makes me feel safe, Boy," she said, "and in control. I want to keep it." She laughed a laugh I'd never heard before—without the tinkle. "It's a fair trade. You get to keep your sister."

This bewildered me. "What do you mean?"

"Well, it's not many woman who have to live with their lover's sister when they move in together."

"But Amy's in the cottage!" I felt all at sea. This was coming from left field.

She shrugged and rolled her eyes. "It might as well be another room in the house; it's that close and she's in here half the time."

True, the cottage was close, but Amy had been completely respectful of our privacy. She never just walked in the way we had done all of our lives, wanting to be together, to share every thought and experience, nothing ever to hide from each other. Now, she knocked or telephoned first. It seemed to me I'd hardly seen her.

"I've hardly seen her!" I began to say, but stifled the words. That wasn't important to defend right now. I'd never been a contentious person. I didn't want to fight with Cecile—ever. I wanted to live in harmony. But fighting was what we were doing. It was sounding quite a lot like this was a fight—me with my strained unnatural voice, her with the tinkle gone, the kissing stopped.

"I thought you liked Amy."

"I do. But not to live with her."

"I could never ask her to leave. This is her house too. She *gave up* the big house for us."

"Naturally. There's one of her and three of us. Masef, I gather, is just an occasional boarder."

"He's Amy's lover."

"That's not how I read it."

"Really?" Another left fielder. I gazed off, wondering.

"Cecile, I am completely confused and upset by this conversation. I'm going for a run."

"Is a run more important than we are?"

"No, of course not. But it will help to get my head straight. It's getting dark, too."

"If you leave now without finishing our discussion, I won't forgive you. I understand your running is important, but I have to know in my heart that I'm more important."

"You are more important. You know how much I love you. More than anyone or anything. But I am going for a run. Now."

And that's what I did. Without another word.

I didn't want to have to run in the dark and chance an injury.

I could have missed a day. But there was my streak —now six years, three months, two days long!

Maybe it was the mistake of my life to go on that run.

Afterward, our relationship began to disintegrate rapidly. She wouldn't make love with me for days, or even talk to me. Needless to say, we didn't finish the discussion about the gun if she wouldn't even say, pass the salt. It was horrible. I completely blamed myself. I abased myself. I *begged* her to forgive me. Yes, me, Trueboy, the Imperious, begging!

I even said she could keep the gun, I who had vowed never to have such a thing in my house or life. I practically said she could buy more guns if she wanted. That's what I'd come to because of the cessation of her affection, which I had learned to require, to crave. And because of the horrible silence she kept. How does someone do that, just not speak at all, the person you adore, who knows you adore them!

But my letting her keep the gun and begging her to forgive me for going running was nothing. I almost promised I'd ask Amy to leave, thinking, if Amy really is coming between us, maybe she should go. Yes, Cecile, who I'd known less than two months, was more important to me than Amy. A couple of times I came close to beginning the sentence: "Okay, I'll ask Amy to go."

Finally, Cecile forgave me and things seemed better but not "ecstatic," not happy, not the way it was before.

That's okay, I told myself. You have to have fights occasionally. Everybody does. We're only human.

And our love will get deeper as we learn about each other.

But the silent treatment was a real surprise. I just wouldn't have thought it of her. She was the same as ever when we were with others: loving-seeming to me and full of fun. But she clammed up when we were alone. That scared me more because, if she could turn happiness on and off, how would I know when it was real?

The respite was short lived. After less than a week of (comparative) bliss, we fought again. This time about Baby.

Baby didn't seem like a very well child to me. For almost two years old, she didn't do anything. She wasn't curious or interested. She seemed withdrawn. She didn't talk baby talk or respond to attention. She seemed fearful. Luckily, she wasn't a crier, but when she did cry she was inconsolable. I didn't know much about babies, but I'd seen Ito with his and other friends with theirs, and I saw how they were with their infants and it struck me that Cecile wasn't a very loving mother. When people were around, she'd pay some attention to Baby, but she ignored her for hours on end when it was just the two of us and I'm sure it was no different when she was alone, probably worse. I tried to spend time with the poor little thing, carry her around, and talk to her, but I might as well have been with a sack of flour.

One day I was just about to go for a run when Baby, alone in her room in the crib, started to cry. I scooped her up and brought her to Cecile who was sunbathing on the lawn. "Here, honey, Baby needs attention. I'm off on my run."

Cecile was lying on her stomach in a bikini.

"Put her over in the shade. She'll just cry more in the hot sun."

"Okay, but why don't you see if she needs a change or is hungry or something?"

"I will in a minute."

It just seemed so coldhearted of her that she wouldn't take Baby in her arms.

"I'm meeting Dan and Emery for a run and I'm already late."

"Go ahead, darling. What's stopping you?"

"I want you to take Baby. I'm not going to just put her down on the lawn, off by herself, while she's so miserable."

"Oh, very well." She rolled over, sat up and took the child. She held her face up to me for a kiss. "Have a good run."

I started off, but turned back after two blocks having forgotten my watch. The other guys would have their watches, but I wanted my own. A long run, it wouldn't have mattered, but we were meeting at the high-school track to do intervals.

Back home, the lawn was vacated. I could hear Baby crying from within the house.

As I neared the bedrooms, I thought I heard the sound of a slap. It froze me in my stride, then I moved along, grabbed my watch from the bathroom where I'd left it after my shower, and looked into Baby's room where Cecile was changing her.

She looked up at me. I studied her face but couldn't read it. Her total lack of expression was a new expression in itself.

"I forgot my watch," I explained. I was still buckling it on my wrist and I held it up for her to see since she probably couldn't hear me above the screams. I went over and looked at Baby. Her face was flushed from crying, but one side of it looked redder.

I waited until Cecile finished dressing her, then I put Baby in the crib and pulled her away where we could talk in relative quiet.

"Cecile," I said, the words sticking in my throat in giant lumps. "I thought I heard a slap."

She looked at me surprised. "Are you saying I struck my baby?"

I flushed guiltily. "No, no. It's just that . . . I thought . . ."

"I can't believe this."

"I'm glad I heard wrong. But I had to say something. I was so scared."

"You think I'm a child beater?"

"No, I don't. But, if you *were* hitting, Baby I'd want to know so . . . so we could get help for you. That's why I asked."

"I know you don't think I'm a good mother. I can tell by your face sometimes. I just don't want to spoil her. You don't understand. It's been hard being a mother alone. Having to take care of myself and her. Her father dead. I've suffered a lot. Baby and I have both suffered a lot."

"I know. Poor darling. But I'm going to take care of you both from now on. And if you need help about Baby . . ."

"It's so awful that you would think such a cruel thing of me. I thought we were going to be so happy, that all my heartache was over. Now this."

"We will be happy. We are happy."

"You don't love Baby."

"Well, no, I don't, not yet," I said truthfully, being the trueboy that I am. "I can't seem to work up any feelings for her. But I want to. I will love her when I get to know her. I'll be her dad."

"I know it's not easy taking on another man's child, but I thought you loved me enough it didn't matter."

"I do, Cecile! I do!"

Here we were all upset again, fighting. And here I was again, about to go off on a run, guys waiting for me. Well, if this turned into a bad fight, I wouldn't go. I wouldn't go. No, not even for the rest of the day, I wouldn't. I'd miss a day. She was more important. Much more.

Still, even thinking about missing my run made me crazy.

She turned and prostrated herself on the couch, head in hands.

I looked longingly at the door. I knew they'd wait for me. They'd wait maybe ten minutes, extending their warm-up, then they'd begin without me.

I went over to the couch and sat down, feeling like striking the same pose as hers, head in my hands.

I couldn't think of anything to say. I knew she wanted comfort but all I could think of was the guys at the track and how I could still make it.

Baby had quieted down.

There was a knock at the door. "Should I get it?" I asked.

She didn't move. I didn't know if I should get it. It might make her feel I was abandoning her.

Masef walked in with his guitar. He wasn't as scrupulous as Amy about our privacy. "Oh, sorry," he said, hesitating on the threshold. "I thought I saw you off on your run. I was going to entertain Cecile."

Cecile sat up. She looked pretty even when she cried. No red nose, no puffiness. She smiled gently. "It's okay. Come in, Masef. Boy's just going. Go on, sweetheart. What are you waiting for?" She laughed, gave me a kiss on the lips, playfully pushed me off the couch.

I went. Gladly. Yes, I have to say gladly, I went. Relieved as hell, grateful to Masef, I ran off with a high heart. And if I get the silent treatment again, I thought, I'll tell her I'll get Amy to go.

I'll do anything in my power to please her, I vowed. Anything but not run.

FOURTEEN

The next morning, because Cecile had a headache, Baby was in my charge. It wasn't a confirmed headache and could be the onset of another silent treatment, but she had spoken enough to ask me to leave her alone and take care of Baby.

I was trying to be loving to the kid because of my yesterday's promise to be a dad, but I couldn't help feeling resentful toward her since it was because of her we'd fought. Now Baby was coming between us along with Amy and my running. I was in a state of anxiety and suspense about the situation, fearing the silent treatment and the deprivation.

I lugged Baby around in one arm while I did various chores around the house and yard. Amy and I always liked to keep the place looking good and, that being our attitude, the work was ongoing.

It was a cool, misty morning to begin with, but Baby and I heated up as the sun cleared the fog and my activity increased, shedding clothes until I was down to solely jeans, Baby to diapers.

The chores meant a lot of going in and out of the garage for tools and I discovered that one thing Baby did respond to was the garage door opening. I opened it a lot that morning, closing it each trip so as to reopen it again for her later. I would press the automatic opener from afar and the door would go up and Baby would actually become animated, would smile and gurgle and wave her hands.

Maybe she could only respond to big gestures, I thought. Small expressions like smiles, hugs, words went over her head, but the up or down sweep of the garage door was talking her language. She was the happening kind of kid. Maybe what it would take for her to get human would be even bigger performances —jet planes landing, construction sites, stock-car races. In this way, the kid could come into her own.

Chores done, I decided to wash the old Volvo, which was in the garage so that meant opening the door again. I decided to set Baby aside while I got the car out, hooked up the hose, got the bucket and cloth. Then I could bring her back to participate. Car washing meant mud. Every kid loved mud.

I set her over on the lawn while I got organized. We didn't have a playpen for her yet because if she did move, she moved so slowly—more a squirm than a crawl and half the time in circles—there was no danger. The yard was big and safe, the level grass becoming field ascending to a wood of young trees before hitting the fence and the road. She would just sit or lie where she was put, not moving except to roll over by mistake and not even wonder about it. I placed her so she could see the garage door.

I don't know how much time passed before I pulled the car out. It must have been more than I realized. Maybe I used up time puttering in the garage before I got in the car. I did shift some things around, steadied some piles.

Backing out, I hit her.

I drove over her.

I felt it, thought it was the bucket of soap and water I'd left standing out ready to hand.

I braked. Pulled forward. Got out.

I couldn't believe it. I just stood there frozen. I kept thinking, call the ambulance, but knew it was useless, hopeless. One only had to see the sight, the mash. No sense even going for a pulse. Call the ambulance! The next thing I knew, Cecile was beside me looking at Baby then me, Baby then me, her eyes huge.

She disappeared. She's calling the ambulance, I thought. She returned a minute later with the gun, the gun we'd fought about. Was she going to shoot me? She should. But why make her a murderer? I'll do it. I think I took the gun. The gun was in my hands. Her eyes were huge. I could have fallen into them.

Then someone took the gun from me. It was Amy. Amy was there now. And Masef.

Then ambulance. Police. I still stood in the place. No one could move me. I was rooted. Rigid. I'd turned into a tree. Someone gave me a shot.

FIFTEEN

It was ten days later when I came to, that I had my
mind again. I was in a hospital bed, an IV dripping
into my arm, Amy sitting by me.

I'd been in a state of catalepsy, she said. Couldn't
hear, talk, move, or speak. Wouldn't eat or drink.

Baby was buried, she said.

Cecile was gone.

When I'd taken in that information, I looked at
Amy. She looked awful. Her eyes looked black and
blue from fatigue and grief. She started to cry. She
dropped her face onto my bed, sobbing my heart out
—her heart. I put my hand gently on her hair, my arm
moving as if on strings. Then I began to cry, too. Our
tears were inexhaustible. "I'm so glad you're back,"
she kept saying. "I thought I'd lost you."

When our tears were shed I looked around and saw
that the room was full of flowers. There was a stack of
cards on my table. "Everyone's called and come to
see you and sent flowers. Time and time again. They
all understand that it was a dreadful accident. They
completely sympathize. We have so many good
friends, Boy. We're lucky."

"Cecile?" My voice was faint and cracked.

Amy shook her head. "She didn't understand. She
would not admit it was an accident. She said you

killed her baby. She said you didn't love Baby, that you'd said as much just the day before. She said all you cared about was your running, not her or Baby. She's gone.

"I'm telling you this to get it said and over, Boy, so you'll know why she left, why she didn't stay by you when you needed her most."

I looked around again. I was in a private room. There was a view of Mt. Tamalpais out the window. Its lovely profile of a sleeping woman was deep purple against the dawn. The sky was pale lavender. A few last stars still twinkled fitfully, hanging on to the night.

I felt crushed by pain. If it was this bad now, how bad must it have been when I couldn't feel it? Enough to kill me I guess. My body saved itself by turning into a tree.

"She was right," came the old man's voice, the ancient wheeze from the bag of bones that was once my winged form. "I loved running more. I'll never run again."

"Yes, you will." Amy resumed her crying. "You will."

"Amy, where's Masef?"

"He's gone, too. I don't know where. He left. Couldn't take it, I guess. I don't blame him. We weren't getting on anyhow. He didn't love me anymore."

"I'm sorry. I'm so sorry, Amy."

"Never mind. I'll be okay now that you're back. We'll both be okay."

I came home a few days later. Once again Amy had fixed the house, removed all traces of Baby and Cecile. She'd repainted the rooms and changed the furniture around so it would all look different to me, be a new beginning. It did. It was transformed. She explained that she'd read this book about Feng Shui: an Ancient Chinese art of placement, a science or way of thinking regarding man's environment that had captured her imagination—how to create balance and harmony in house design and achieve good luck thereby. Feng Shui said that white (the color of all our walls) was not a good color to live in. It was the color of illness and death. So, now the walls were green (health and tranquility), and saffron (wisdom, longevity—the color of Buddhist robes). The house looked extremely odd. But it worked. It helped me from the moment I returned.

There were also mirrors in unexpected places: by the kitchen stove, on a bedroom window, in a passageway. "They avert evil influences as well as keep the good luck flowing around," Amy said. We've got to try everything."

She'd moved back into the house to be with me. The cottage remained empty, white, still with a hole in it, no mirrors—a ghost cottage. We never went in it. We relegated the tragedy to the cottage. It had to go somewhere from the house and yard, from the deep recesses of our hearts.

The first weeks home, Ito came to stay, left his wife and child and came to be with me. My body was still rigid. It was hard to get around and sometimes I'd shake all over from head to toe. How can you be rigid and shaking at the same time? Sometimes Ito carried me.

He massaged me, talked to me, imbued me with his strength. He took me on tiny tottering walks and for swims in the pool of an estate where he gardened. At night he sat by my bed reading me the poems of the hermit monk Ryokan, a man who understood the loneliness, difficulty, and impermanence of life, but celebrated its beauty and sweetness. I guess all great poets notice life as he did, but only a few understand it as he did—only the champions.

"O, that my priest's robe were wide enough
to gather up all the suffering people
In this floating world."
Gradually, I began to heal.

Amy had to feed me with a spoon, slowly, patiently, morsel by morsel because my face was rigid, too. My jaw, tongue, lips, throat, all had trouble going through the motions.

I was skin and bone. My muscles atrophied. A lifetime of running muscles were wiped out in six weeks.

While my face and body lacked all expression, hers incorporated the tragedy. Her eyes brimmed with sorrow. She kept up with her job, the housekeeping, her care of me but looked moment to moment like someone about to faint, cry, scream. She never did.

Masefield came. It was five weeks after the event that he got the news. He'd been in a salt mine in Poland to find an elusive minister of state from another country who was seeking a cure for his asthma. The salt mine worked. White was the color of health for him, said Masefield, the color of being able to breathe.

He came, he saw, gave us money, and went. He couldn't stay and help. It was not his way. What he had to do was go and find out.

"Where has Cecile gone?" he wanted to know. "Where is Masef?"

Three months later, a day in late August, I was mowing the lawn when I heard the phone ring above the clatter of the blades. When I told the person Amy wasn't home and replaced the receiver, I realized I'd run to the phone. My body, without asking me, impelled by the ringing, had run.

I felt overcome by a yearning for the life I had led as a runner. I remembered my life before Cecile as an idyll, a time of joy and freedom and challenge not found anywhere. Yes, *before* was the happy time—the time of practice. I glimpsed that truth, but only momentarily because it paled before the red-hot memory of being a hero and lover, of being a champion.

I couldn't run again. It would be too callous. It would be unforgivable. Even if I ran privately, just for myself, never to race others, it would be unspeakable.

Running would make me feel good again, possibly even happy, but I had no right to feel that way. I had killed an infant, my lover's infant. My lover, now, wherever she was, suffered ongoing, insupportable (as Amy would say) grief. So must I.

I missed Cecile so much. Sometimes I fantasized that she returned and forgave me, that we had a child together, that I ran in the Olympics, took the Gold for America.

Why did I torment myself? It would never happen.

I could only run again with her permission, with her forgiveness. Even with that beneficent go-ahead, I wouldn't race. Because all the world knew of Baby's death. Such a man would not be permitted to represent America. Nor should he be.

Even if people believed it was an accident—which they never would because of Cecile leaving me.

The inquest brought in a verdict of accidental

death, but afterward she'd told the press I didn't love
Baby. That I loved running more. It would seem de-
cent of her that she didn't say so at the inquest but, in
fact, her saving it until after made it appear she had
withheld evidence, that she knew more than she was
telling, and it branded me. I was still in the hospital at
the time. She said I'd lost my mind so I wouldn't have
to face the truth.

She only said such a thing out of her own heart-
break. I know she didn't believe it in her heart. But it
was said and done and I stood convicted as a human
being.

I did love running more than baby, but if anyone
said to me, choose between Baby's life and never running again, I'm sure I would have chosen Baby's life.

Just now I ran to the phone. Involuntarily, I ran.
What if it happened again, for longer and longer dis-
tances? What if I started running in my sleep? Or
became a secret runner, doing it behind my own
back?

I remembered my life as a runner. My feet remembered the mountain trails, every root and rock of
them, in rain, fog, or sun, at every turn, rise, and fall
of their spiderweb embrace of the mountain's terrain:
Ocean View Trail, Matt Davis, Coastal, Dipsea, Rock
Springs, Old Mine, Cataract, Fern Creek, Miller the
Killer.

Tears came to my eyes. I brushed them away. It was
only self-pity, which was vile.

I remembered the feel of a shower after a long,
hard run, the taste of food, the nectar of spring water
in the middle of a hot day's twenty-miler. I remembered running alone like an Indian through the intensely timeless Redwood forest or the ineffable joy
and bonding of running with a comrade mile upon

mile, two hearts beating as one, footfalls in synch, breathing together, talking without pretense or calculation as easy as breathing—shooting the breeze.

My days as a freeling. Now I was a cagedling. And so I would remain. Serving time.

I went to the wall of those quotes by others who had been similarly, gloriously possessed. It had stood unregarded since Baby's death.

The known and memorized quotes flashed through my mind's eye like the beloved visages of friends. How they had nourished me, inspired me, goaded me through sinking spells, applauded my achievements.

Approaching it, the first quote I sighted was one by Jean–Claude Killy: "There have aways been certain dangers, always certain risks, but that only meant I must work harder, do more things, ski more difficult runs. For I always told myself from the beginning, 'If you are a skier, you must ski.' "

Oh, yes, but who could imagine the danger of killing a child, Jean–Claude, and losing your lover, all in one blow, your body growing rigid as a phone pole and being condemned by all but your sister and closest friends as a murderer, condemned even by yourself. Then you can't run any more. Then, not running, you are no longer a runner, hardly a man.

Above the quotes hung my crown of laurel, an ever-withering wreath, crackley and sere. Like I was.

I'll go back to school. Yes, I better see what I can learn. It's time to leave.

I wonder if this is a house of ill luck. What if Sister is in a danger that all her Feng Shui colors and mirrors can't avert.

Ha! What could happen to Amy worse than already has? She is in fact a tower of strength, a survivor, a

life-giver and strength-giver to her brother. I would
be twice, three times dead without her.

I remembered with a thrill of horror how in my
passion for Cecile, I had considered asking Amy to
leave home so we could have the whole, huge place
to ourselves. Cecile wanted that and I was almost willing to do it to make her happy, to make her be loving
to me in the way she had first shown.

What if I had not run that day? What if I had said at
once that, of course, I would ask Amy to go? Would
everything be different? Would I have had it be different on those terms?

How much do you do for your loved one? How far
do you go?

Amy used to say that one day I'd marry and my
family would necessarily be more important to me
than she.

But if you love a runner, do you ask him not to
run? If you love a man who loves his sister, do you
ask him to send her away?

Forget it. What does it matter when the immutable
fact is that I killed her baby.

*"I never for a day gave up listening to the songs of
birds . . ."*

I tried to turn the cut-down wall of quotes to the
wall of my bedroom, but hadn't the strength. Instead,
I got out a tablecloth and hung it over the wall. The
linen was the color of illness and death and being able
to breathe.

SIXTEEN

Masefield looked for the deserters of Boy and Amy. He wasn't satisfied with the situation. He felt uneasy. He felt that Masef, abandoning Amy in her time of trouble, had behaved out of character. He remembered that when he was young, he'd behaved similarly with Masef's mother, abandoning her because he thought he had something more important to do.

So, whenever he had time to himself, he searched. But months went by and he couldn't find a trace of either Cecile or Masef. He wasn't too surprised that he couldn't find his son. After all, he was a master at disappearing himself and he had taught Masef all his tricks. But he was very surprised that he hadn't found Cecile. That should have taken two days, tops. As a result he could only conclude that the two deserters were together. Masef must have thought it was more important to be with Cecile. He must have thought he was in love with her. That was the only thing that could make being with her in her trouble more important than sticking by Amy.

If they were together, and he believed they were, it cast a whole new light, a harsh light. They might have already formed a plan of running off together. She had a history of leaving dead bodies in her path. Could she have been involved in baby's accident unbeknownst to Boy?

Masefield asked his staff to trace down the circumstances of Cecile's husband's death, but nothing could be found. He got a read-out of all the deaths by violence in the United States during the time of her pregnancy, but there were too many. He looked into baby deaths. Infant mortality was on the upswing in the country because of all the dope-addicted mothers. There were thousands.

Duncan Rodd was in a meeting, but Masefield insisted his card be sent into the man knowing that would blast him out of there in about two seconds. Anyone in government knew the name Masefield, and this wouldn't be too different than the president requesting a moment of his time—or the attorney general. Masefield had the power J. Edgar Hoover used to have, only his, he liked to think, was a power for good not evil. The comparison was apt, however, because he, like Hoover, knew more about kingpins than they knew themselves. It kept people on their toes around him. Rodd would be peeing his pants. But Masefield didn't know Rodd's secrets. He wasn't interested.

"I'm trying to locate your daughter, Cecile," Masefield said at once. The man was wiping his brow. He was overweight and florid-faced. Masefield figured he'd be dead in about two and a half years.

"Haven't heard a thing from her since she went West with the marathoner," Rodd said.

Masefield waited.

"Not a thing. Really. She never did keep in touch." There was bitterness to his tone. "She'd only come home when she was out of money. Then she'd act like she'd been the loving daughter all along. And I'd be taken in every time, end up making a big fuss over her, give her anything she asked for." He shook his head.

Masefield waited.

"She had bad luck with men. Always said if she could find someone like her Daddy she'd be okay." He shook his head again, not believing it.

"Did you know her husband?"

"Never met him. Come to think of it, I don't even know his name."

"How did he die?"

"Gun-cleaning accident, according to Cecile. He was a gun nut. But so am I for that matter." He chuckled. "So's Cecile."

"She was pregnant at the time. Do you think there were other children—maybe another child who might have died in the . . . accident?"

"Funny you should ask because my wife thought she had another kid. Got all upset that Cecile had had her grandchild and never told her. But Cecile was always so secretive. And when she did tell things, half the time her stories never hung together, almost like she couldn't tell truth from falsehood. Didn't know the difference. I personally think she never was married to a guy who got killed, that she invented the whole thing to explain the baby she was carrying and get pity instead of condemnation." He ground his teeth for having been suckered once again. "I wouldn't have let her in our home if she'd been knocked up by some guy, but a widow's another story."

No one *ever* asked Masefield a question. This man did. "Do you have a kid?"

Masefield didn't answer.

"They sure can tear your heart out, can't they?"

"I don't know," Masefield said. So far Masef

hadn't. But when he thought about him lately he was conscious of a worry in his heart which was turning into an ache as the investigation wore on. He hadn't been happy with his nephew loving this woman. At the thought of his son loving her, he was wretched. When he thought of his sweet-natured son and this woman with the reptilian glance, who was older than him by maybe ten years, then yes, there was a feeling of his heart being torn. When he thought of her acquaintance with murder, he felt a fear that he had never in his life felt for himself and only one other time felt for Masef, the time he was lost at sea. Laurie had found him then. Maybe Laurie could find him now. Laurie knew him the best of all. For himself, he was stymied. The only place to go now was back to the start. He returned to Marin.

"I could have assumed it was like all his other trips and that he'd be back," Amy told Masefield. "Because he promised to tell me if he ever found another home. And he didn't take his motorcycle; it's still here. He took his fishing rod and guitar, but he almost always did. I have no reason to think he won't be back except that he . . . did seem to have stopped loving me when he left. In my heart, I feel I've lost him. But I know I haven't given up hope."

It was mid-December. Amy, Masefield, and Ito sat in the yard on a balmy afternoon waiting for Boy to arrive from Berkeley for the weekend. He'd returned to college in September and was pretty well recovered, except for occasional bouts of trembling and except for the fact that he still didn't run and wasn't going to. His wall of quotes remained shrouded.

"Masef suffers," Ito said. "Such restlessness as Amy describes, is a disease."

Both Masefield and Amy were startled. Being used to Masef's ways, they seemed normal.

"It doesn't constitute an unwholesome mind, but definitely a stained mind," Ito said.

Ito's skin tones seemed to soak up the rays of the lowering sun and glow with them. His energy blasted away in the open space, dissipating at about fifty yards. Masefield, in contrast, looked old, tired, pale, but nonetheless powerful. His power didn't blast, it seeped.

Amy was the most upset at Ito's remark. Masef always appeared to be so happy and she assumed his travelling was part of the fun he had in living (once she knew it wasn't business). Now it occurred to her that maybe he went away when he no longer could appear to be happy. Maybe he had times of inconsolable, insupportable sadness when he had to be off by himself alone. She remembered Laurie maintaining he was emotionally crippled and how she had scorned the remark.

Masefield also was thoughtful, his paternal pride warring with his respect for Ito's words. He said to Amy, "Weren't you surprised that he would leave you and Boy at such a tragic time?"

"I was surprised," Amy admitted. "And hurt. But, as you both know, things had been bad between us."

Masefield recapitulated. "Boy met Cecile in early April. They returned here in early May. It was about five weeks later that she left. Masef left the same time."

"That's right," Amy said. "June 10. It's been seven months. He's never been gone that long before. I wonder if Laurie's heard from him? I wonder if he went to see her before he left? He always did. To

assure her, he said, because she had such a huge fear
of losing him, going back to when they were kids."

Masefield lit a cigarette. Amy wished he wouldn't.
He looked so old to her today. So weary and gaunt.
She realized he was fifty now, maybe older. She realized he'd die some day and the thought was insupportable. She wished he'd take care of himself, not
smoke. *People die,* she thought woefully. *That's what
life is. It's horrible. It's not fair. I'm going to lose everyone
and then I'll lose myself. Down into "the grave wither thou
goest."*

That'll be a passage, all right, she thought. *That'll be a
hole with a cover on top. I see why Masefield likes the quote.
It makes life's holes bearable, even interesting.*

"I didn't expect to find Masef," he was saying, "so
practiced is he in evaporating, but finding Cecile
should have been a cinch. This points to something,
Amy."

Amy had no idea what it pointed to.

"I think they're together," Masefield said. He
looked at his watch and went on speaking so Amy
could collect herself. "I hope Boy gets here before
dark. I've also asked Laurie to come by. I hope that's
okay. I thought we should all put our heads together."

Amy recovered enough to ask, falteringly, "Masefield, why do you think Cecile and Masef are together?"

"Because they left the same day and I can't find
either of them. Suppose she asked him to take her
away? It would explain his abandoning you in your
trouble since she was in worse trouble. It's the only
explanation."

"But it was me he loved! We were a couple!"

Masefield pressed his lips together as if trying to

restrain the words he had to say. "Masef was very taken with her right from the start."

"So what? Everyone was."

"Even before he met her. When he saw her on the marathon tape, crowning Boy. He kept looking at her picture. He was mesmerized."

"Was she the woman who crowned Boy?" Ito asked.

"Yes. That's how they met."

Ito closed his eyes and breathed deeply, remembering the darkness he'd seen at the moment of their meeting.

"Let's hand wrestle," Masefield said to Ito. He lit up with the saying of it, shedding thirty years, looking like Masef, full of fun. "And Amy can take on the winner."

The three gloomy people were galvanized. They ran, almost merrily, to the backyard. Amy was thinking, *I can't throw either of these men into the pond. Especially not Masefield. It would be like hand wrestling God. And when Ito goes in, it will cause a tidal wave that might endanger the house!*

She didn't notice that she assumed whoever she took on would be vanquished by her, that it didn't occur to her she could lose—even to God.

The men stripped down to their shorts, Masefield, long, lean and wiry, Ito like a block of granite. They began. It was a strained, silent, interminable time before Ito was unbalanced. He fell into the pond with a rebounding splash. Masefield hardly had time to gloat because Amy took her position and it was only an instant, a split second, before Masefield joined Ito among the water lilies, having succumbed to the master hand wrestler herself.

"Rematch!" Masefield called, struggling out of the

water, astonished and dismayed. "I want a rematch!" But Amy had run away to the front of her house, so horrified was she by what she had done. So pleased!

"I don't get it, Ito," Masefield turned bewildered, purple eyes to his old friend, looking helpless for the first time in years, his black curls slicked to his head, a pink lily askew on his shoulder, "What did she do? How did she do it, that slip of a girl!"

"She hath shewed strength with her arm," Ito replied in full, round tones, "she hath scattered the proud in the imagination of their hearts, she hath put down the mighty . . ."

"Tell it not in Gath," cried Masefield, the hurt and ignominy of his loss dispersed by the marvelous words. "Publish it not in the streets of Askelon . . ."

". . . lest the daughters of the philistines rejoice," they orated in unison. "Lest the daughters of the uncircumcised triumph . . ."

"Hey, guys," Amy called, breaking up the biblical exchange between the two drenched men, "Boy's here."

Boy had left the Volvo at the bottom of the driveway, as was his custom since the accident, and walked up to the house. He looked fine. Some might say he looked better than he had as a runner, more normal looking. But that was what was sad—that he was so normal, that he no longer carried himself with the heroic grace and majesty of one who would be an Olympian. Gone was the radiance. Gone the steel. Gone, too, the assured way of speaking, bordering on imperious. Now, he was like anyone else, hair cut short, body filled out. Except he still moved stiffly. As if it were his bones that had been broken, not his spirit.

SEVENTEEN

The wondrous house and my three loved ones all presented themselves before a sunset that reached pastel fingers into half the sky. The other half held swollen clouds that might contain rain or just be posing there before rolling off out of the sky.

Ito and Masefield appeared from the backyard, pulling on clothes. Amy brought a towel for Masefield's wet head. Ito's was shaved but he passed the towel over it anyhow. They looked like a couple of young rowdies as they greeted me. Then the years settled back over them. They grew grave.

Ito asked me for the car keys. I watched him go down the driveway for the Volvo. He drove it up and parked it in the garage for the first time since the accident. Then he came out and shut the door, returning the keys to me. I was bewildered.

Masefield fixed me with an imperative eye. "I'm going to ask a terrible thing of you. I'm going to ask you to recreate the death of Baby. I want you to go through all the motions you went through from the moment you set Baby down on the lawn. I know you've relived it a thousand times in your mind. Now I want it reenacted. Amy. I want you to be Baby."

"What . . . what do you mean? What do I do?"

"I want you to crawl, as Baby did, toward the place

she was hit. You remember her crawling style and
speed?"

"Yes."

"Bear in mind how much smaller than you she was
and move accordingly."

"Boy?" Ito asked.

"Yes?"

"Do you remember how you used to move?" His
voice was gentle, but his eye no less imperative than
Masefield's. "It was quick and assured," he reminded
me. "Your every move was economical. It was beautiful to behold. Try to move that way now."

"Let's go," Masefield said.

I obeyed blindly, unquestioningly, caught up in the
exercise. I took Amy to a spot on the lawn, about
thirty feet from the driveway. "I figure Baby didn't
start crawling until she saw the door go up," I said
haltingly.

"But you don't know," Masefield said. "So, Amy,
start now. You, too, Boy."

Amy put all her heart into the idea of being Baby,
paying no attention to the others. She got it in her
mind to head straight for the garage, although at grass
level it was almost beyond her (Baby's) powers to get
a fix. She remembered how, when trying to crawl,
she'd half the time roll over, then be all confused
about where she was and where she was going—not
that it ever mattered. Amy/Baby was determined not
to roll over and get confused. It mattered to her to
get to the driveway. She would be like an athlete and
go beyond her powers. With this mindset, she kept to
her incremental squirm across the green, making a
beeline for the garage.

Meanwhile, I got going on my part. The sun was

setting and the light wouldn't hold much longer. I put my mind back to that hot summer morning.

"I walked into the kitchen to fill the bucket," I was talking to myself as well as to Masefield and Ito, leaving them while I entered the house.

Where was Cecile? Had I seen her? Had I poked my head into the bedroom? No, the door had been closed and I figured she was asleep, curing her headache.

I returned to the yard with the bucket full of soapy water.

"I'm sure I would have glanced over at Baby to see she was still in place," I said to Masefield and Ito as I put the bucket down.

"Just assume for now that you didn't, that you forgot her. What did you do next?"

"I hooked up the hose," I gestured to the valve near the front door. "It was in the backyard," I said, going to get it, returning to screw it on to the faucet. I told them, "Masef or Amy was in the shower. I could hear the water and I remember figuring they'd be through by the time I needed the hose."

Opening the garage door with the control button, I strained to avoid looking back at the yard to see how far Baby had come.

I began to feel anxious, moving with no economy of motion, but with major clumsiness. As I entered the garage, my anatomy began to tremble, my first attack of the shakes in weeks.

I recreated the few fiddling things I'd done in the garage before getting in the car: restacking some paint cans, moving a few boxes.

Finally, pouring with perspiration, I got in the car. I was unable to put the key in the ignition, so unsteady was my hand. I watched in fascination, hypnotized by the little clicking Morse-code sound of key hitting the hole. Ito came over to the window, reached in and inserted it for me. Then I started the engine, backed out of the garage, braked.

Like an old man, I crawled out of the car.

It was a tableau in the dying light of day. Masefield and Ito were dead still. They stood over on the lawn, looking down at the body of Amy being Baby. She had covered not quite half the distance.

For me, it was as if I came alive from the dead. All the feelings that had been dormant in me thrust through like flowers blooming out of the desiccated cracks of the desert floor after a burst of rain. I felt love, happiness, hope. God did I feel hope. I ran to Amy, leaned over and pulled her to her feet shouting, laughing. "I didn't do it, Amy! Oh God, God, maybe I didn't do it. Look! You're only half way. Not even half way!"

Then of course I realized I did do it. This was just a mock-up. In real life, the car had gone over Baby but . . . but . . .

Amy was just as excited. Talking a mile a minute, she spluttered. "I'm sure I moved faster than Baby would have. Well, maybe not faster, but more determinedly. You know how she never could go on course. She never could go anywhere except in circles, really. Why didn't we think of this? Where were our minds! Oh, Boy! Boy!"

We started dancing across the lawn, whirling like two dervishes. We whooped and hollered. We laughed and careened around.

Ito watched us with a small, sad, smile on his face, but Masefield looked stunned and just kept saying "M . . . M . . ." his hands out gropingly like a blind man.

Suddenly, he seemed to go berserk. Yes, Masefield, the master of cool, the man who could teach kings imperturbability—Asian kings—went berserk. He pulled us apart. He yelled at us. "Stop! Stop! We're not finished. There's more to learn. Much more."

In the grip of my maniacal, illusory relief, I shouted back, "No! No! It's true. I didn't kill Baby. In my heart, I knew all the time that it couldn't have happened as it did. Now, I know. I know!"

"We don't know!" Masefield shouted and he began to shake me as if he were angry with me, as if he wanted to hurt me. And he was hurting me. I cried out.

Ito pulled Masefield away from me. "Stop," he said to him. "Look at yourself."

"You don't understand," Masefield said and made another lunge for me.

Ito did something, it was hard to see what, but Masefield fell to the ground, fell flat on his face, and lay there, stunned. "I do understand," Ito said.

Then Amy went over and started pummelling away at Ito, like a butterfly beating its wings against a tree.

I couldn't believe it?

It was incredible.

We were all behaving like lunatics.

Then I had to leap to pull Amy away from Ito, feeling horribly upset that she would show hostility to him, the best of me. Why were we all beating up on each other, getting so mad—me now mad at Amy, feeling blind outrage about her attack on Ito.

"Masefield just freaked because he's afraid Masef was involved in Baby's death," Amy hotly defended him to Ito, struggling in my arms.

"No, he's not," Ito said calmly. "That's not it."

"But Masef was with me," she assured Masefield,

ignoring Ito's remark, getting free of me and leaning over to give him a hand up, for he was still prostrate on the grass. "He was getting out of the shower when I came in from the darkroom."

Masefield unsteadily regained his feet, saying something that sounded like rematch.

"Then Masef and I were together *the whole time* until we heard Boy's cry," she said.

"Please," Masefield begged, spreading his arms, wavering on his long legs, "let's continue."

"We are continuing," she told him. "We're saying what happened next."

"Oh."

He was still dazed.

"Amy, did you say you heard me cry?" I asked.

"Yes, it was a horrible keening sound. A thin wail. We couldn't imagine what it was. That's why we came running. And thank God we did, since you were standing there with the gun and who knows what might have happened next."

"Gun?" Masefield clutched his brow. "Gun!"

"I'd forgotten that," I said. "The gun. I'd completely forgotten."

"How did a gun get into all this?" Ito wondered aloud.

"Cecile ran inside," I told them. "She came back with her gun. Maybe she gave it to me, but I think I took it from her so I could shoot myself and not have to live another minute with the horror of what had happened. I can't believe I did live."

I looked all around as if for an answer to how I'd lived.

"I'm sorry, Ito," Amy said, kissing him impulsively. "Please forgive me."

"It was nothing. I hardly felt it. You see, I had to

fell Masefield to intruct him, to alert him. He was letting his fear unbalance him."

"Fear?" Amy and I asked in unison. "Masefield?"

Masefield made another hopeless attempt to get us back into the re-creation. Amy again told him we were continuing and again he said "Oh." We asked Ito about Masefield's fear since he was now the man in charge, Masefield being out of it, even about his own fear, and Ito explained, "He is completely terrified because Masef is with this woman."

"He's not with her," Amy said. "We don't know that for sure. I just know he's not. He can't be."

"But what is it Masefield fears for Masef if she is?" I asked. "I don't understand."

Ito said, "Clearly, Baby couldn't have covered all that distance in the time she had to do so, even if it was within her powers. We ask ourselves, what did happen? It's possible that this woman is an anomaly, an exceptionally evil person who purposely put her baby down for the Volvo to strike."

"No," I said. "It's unthinkable."

"Boy, why do you think we did this test?" said Masefield, who had sat down in a garden chair and was beginning to sound like himself. "This woman leaves dead people in her path and comes out a winner, getting all the sympathy and support, as well as the drama and attention she obviously craves." We all listened, riveted by his stern, uncompromising tone. "I think she killed her last husband and maybe another baby, too. She didn't succeed in killing you, but she partially destroyed you."

"But you don't know this," I said quietly. "You're . . . you're guessing."

"That's right. And it will be hard to prove. But we'll try."

"If it's true," Ito put his arm around me, "you're free."

"If it's true," Masefield said heavily, "Masef will be her next victim."

"Only if he's with her," Amy said defiantly. "Let's go inside," Amy said. "We're all standing here in the dark. It's pitch dark out here."

It was. Night had fallen like a curtain going down. We could hardly see each other.

EIGHTEEN

"Let's have a drink," Amy switched on the lights as she went through the house. "I'll get the cognac. And I better get out a case of beer for when Laurie comes."

Laurie's voice came from a deep wicker chair on the indoor porch that fronted the house. She sat, beer in hand, a six pack by her side. "I brought my own, thanks, since I already know how long it takes to get a drink around this place. Plus, I didn't want to interrupt the free-for-all on the lawn." She blinked as the lights went on. "Hey, what happened to the house? It looks like goddamn Chinatown around here."

She stood up in an easy seamless motion, the way I used to get out of a deep chair, like levitating. She was wearing black jeans and boots, a white tank top, no bra. Her skin was uniformly brown, darker than Ito's. Her hair was black and slippery with more light and movement to it than her face, which was like those old sepia photos one sees of American Indians —prematurely ancient, the eyes full of all the experiences that still lay ahead.

"This is Boy," Masefield introduced her. "And Ito."

"I'm sorry about your tragedy," she said straight-forwardly. It made me like her right away. Other peo-

ple avoided the subject, avoided me, too. If I hadn't
achieved that modicum of fame from the marathon
just before it happened, maybe the papers wouldn't
have made so much of it but I did, and they did, and
everyone knew the story. Then there'd been the interview with Cecile and I became a pariah. I looked as
bad as a man could look and still walk around free.
When I finally left home to go to Berkeley, it had
been hard to walk around normally, not skulk around
like a whipped dog.

"Thank you," I said to Laurie. I almost hugged her.
I was feeling so elated from what had just happened.
Then, meeting this down-to-earth woman seemed to
bring me back from the dead.

"Ito, I've heard of you," she said shaking his hand.
"You're a hotshot gardener in the county. I'm in the
same business, only I do the shit work. Clear out
blackberries and poison oak. Haul stuff to the dump."

Ito nodded.

"You do nice gardens," she said. "Tranquil. Radi-
ant."

I could see Amy was getting pissed off at the good
impression Laurie was making. I hoped there wasn't
going to be another lunatic free-for-all of fiercely con-
tending loyalties.

But no, Amy passed around snifters of cognac. She
had naturally good conduct and anyone who was a
guest in her house got treated courteously.

We settled on the porch, since that's where Laurie
already was. There was a lounge, plenty of chairs, a
piano that nobody played. I guess Mom used to.
Through the windows I could see a gibbous moon
had squeezed between two of the fat clouds, as if to
illumine the yard for Laurie as Masefield explained
what we'd just done.

He told her about our re-creation of the crime. Yes, crime. I still had to integrate this new knowledge. All kinds of memories were flooding my mind now, the way Cecile was with Baby: the fact she didn't name her, the way she only showed affection to her in front of other people, but very soon gave up the pantomime in front of me, treating Baby like a doorstop. That vision came to me because one day she actually did put Baby down to hold the door while she was going in and out. And many other things came to mind that I had allowed, tolerated, not acknowledged. Except the slap. Thank God, I at least confronted her on that . . . even though I backed down like a miserable cur at the first sign of her crocodile tears.

Laurie listened stony-faced to Masefield's recapitulation. Her reaction was the same as his. "M's in danger."

"*If* he's with Cecile, as I suspect."

"He is. She was with him when he came to say goodbye. I promised I wouldn't tell."

Amy looked stricken. "You were probably nice to her, too," she said bitterly, "feeling so glad he was leaving me."

"I guess I can be nice to a woman who's kid has just been killed."

Amy continued relentlessly, "Probably you were going to wait until she'd done grieving before you went to wreck her home. Then later you could start sending her death threats."

"All right, all right," Laurie shouted at Amy. "So, I'm a fuckhead. So, I'm sorry."

Ito smiled.

"What's so funny?" Laurie asked him, glaring all around.

"You remind me of me when I was young."

"Well, maybe there's hope for me then," Laurie grumbled. She finished her beer and cracked another.

"You begin by giving up attachment," Ito turned on her the fullness of his gaze. "Stop clinging."

"Are you kidding? Clinging is my middle name."

"Laurie, have you talked to Masef since?" Masefield asked intently, getting back to the main subject.

"Once. About three months ago. He asked how you guys were. I told him everything sucked. He called from a booth, but I have no idea where. You can always tell a booth, though. Traffic sounds and stuff."

"How did he sound?" Amy asked.

"He didn't say anything about himself, just asked about other people."

"Think back, Laurie," Masefield asked. "Did he give any clue as to where he was?"

We were all silent. She shook her head. Then she stood up. "I'll go stake out Buster's grave. He hasn't been there yet. I've checked. But he'll come eventually. I'll go right now and wait until he comes."

"That could be months. What about your life?"

"Masef is my life," she said simply. "And when he comes," she promised, "I'll tell him about your suspicions and beg him not to go back to her. Hell, I won't let him go back to her. I'll hog-tie him."

After she left, Amy said wearily to the rest of us, "He said he'd tell me when our house was no longer his home. I guess he lied." She had the look on her face I'd seen so many times since June—of trying not to cry.

"Masef's a fool. He's always been a fool." This from his father. "But, Amy, don't blame him. Seducing Masef away from you was just part of Cecile's whole grim crime against the family.''

All these months, Amy had never expressed her sadness over the lost Masef. How could she? It was such a minor grief compared to mine.

"To think I blamed Laurie when all along it was Cecile wrecking my relationship. I think her seduction of Masef began way before the baby's death. Maybe as soon as she got here."

Ito said, "If only I'd warned Boy. I had dark feelings about her."

"It wouldn't have done any good," I said. "I was too infatuated." Again, I remembered almost-throwing-out-Amy.

"If only he'd said goodbye," Amy said, "I could have asked him not to go. But I never could teach him to say goodbye."

At last she began to cry. She kept on crying for hours, long after Ito and Masefield had gone. She cried away the trying-not-to-cry expression and I never saw it again.

In the following days, and months, she took on an almost unrealistically positive attitude, convinced that between Laurie and Masefield, Masef would be "home" momentarily. This occasioned another gigantic house cleaning and she adorned the place with more flowers than ever before—bouquets and plants —increased twofold by the ubiquitous Feng Shui mirrors.

In January, Amy said she no longer felt as if Masef were coming, but almost as if he were already arrived. She said she seemed to hear the music of his guitar in the dark and wintry air.

In February, she stopped talking about him. But I knew she still waited.

As for me, I didn't expect him. They were both lost to us, maybe dead. Yes. I began to think that was why they couldn't be found. Because they were dead.

How long would Laurie and Amy wait, one at the grave, one here. How long would Masefield search?

I was the only one who went on with my life, my half-life.

NINETEEN

Laurie made camp a quarter of a mile from Buster's grave in a hollow beneath the wildly gesturing orange limbs of an ancient madrone. As Masef wouldn't be coming to Buster's grave at night, she could sleep at her mother's in Inverness or at Sunny's little house that sat out on pilings on Tomales Bay, but she often chose to sleep at her camp, enjoying being alone. She had a sleeping bag, foam pad, tent, kerosene cookstove, cooler, lots of warm but lightweight clothing she could layer up in since it was now March; when the temperatures veered from low seventies to high thirties and when it rained it poured.

She'd put her hauling business in the hands of a friend and took just enough income from it to get by. Work was slow, anyhow, at this time of year so she wouldn't miss much.

On this day, the day she finally saw Masef, she'd been almost three months at the stakeout.

At first, she'd felt anxious, impatient, unhappy, lonely, angry, self-pitying. But as the days passed, she felt better, then good, then often inexplicably happy.

Each morning, she went for a long horseback ride, early enough that she wouldn't fret about missing Masef if he came, watching the dawn pull night's drapes off the green-gold land, the azure sea. If it was raining, she'd watch it lighten to day by monochrome shades, as she galloped through the watery dark, the cobalt, the grey, then the light.

The Point Reyes National Seashore had endless trails and there were all the West Marin ranchlands to traverse as well.

She'd tether the horse at her camp, groom and feed it, then make a big breakfast for herself. She'd settle in for the day with her binoculars at the ready, her twenty-two also at the ready to bag any small game scampering by, and plenty of books at her side. Most of the time she found herself contented with her own thoughts.

She thought about her maternal grandfather Bart, a full-blooded Blackfoot. Her mother talked about him on nights she spent at home. In his youth, he'd been a fine cowboy and he ran the rodeo circuit, busting broncs, roping steer, taking prizes. Those were his good years. Then he became a drunk and a crazy. In his crazy years, he gave up living in a house to wander the roads dementedly, camping different places at night. He didn't have all this gear that she had, no Patagonia for him. He wore an old black woolen coat with a rope tied around the waist. He had a tin pot to boil water in and a rifle to shoot game to cook over his fire on a stick.

He had certain places he'd always camp—about five different places, so her mom said, that were uncannily wonderful. It was as if the memory of Indian lore that lodged in his collective unconscious came to the fore when all his socialized behavior departed, so fine-tuned was his sense for picking the right site, that both gave protection and supplied a view, that had a quality of air and light which transformed the landscape around him, as well as the tormented terrain inside his skin.

"The poor old man must have felt at peace at least once or twice when he was alone in some of those locations," her mom said. "I hope so."

Laurie, in the months of camping near Buster's grave, had felt peace once or twice. Maybe three times. Which was three times more than she ever had before.

The reason this came up about her grandfather was that the site Laurie had picked to make camp was one of his.

It seemed to heighten her senses. She knew she could see farther today than when she first came to settle here in the sight of Buster's grave. And the other senses, too, seemed dizzyingly sharp. Of course, it could be because she wasn't drinking so much. She hoped not. She'd hate to have to choose between the good feeling she got from drinking and this one of the sharpened senses. She'd like to have both.

Maybe putting my butt on horseflesh and earth all day is bringing out the Indian in me, Laurie thought. *Mom always said I was a throwback anyhow, being so much darker than she. I just hope I won't be thrown back to the alcoholism and craziness, too. Amy would say I already had been. She'd say that on that score I'm ahead of Bart by twenty years. Well, Amy just brings out the worst in me. She's so fair and pretty and nice, so together. She keeps her house so fine and has so many friends. Not to mention the overwhelming good luck of M loving her—wanting to live with her, anyhow. Granted, he was bewitched by Cecile, but he sure was happy with Amy. She understood him, Amy did. She let him be.*

She could be generous in her mind to Amy now that Amy'd lost M to another. Amy was worse off than she was now as far as M was concerned because M would always keep in touch with her. After all, they'd grown up together, inside each other's pockets. Other women would come and go, but she would always be there for him, always be the last one he'd see before going somewhere and who knows, maybe one day, he wouldn't go, he'd stay and they'd finally be together the way they were meant to be.

Laurie thought she saw movement on the knoll that was distinguished from the others by a carnival of flowers and shrubs from the almost twenty years of M's planting them there by Buster's gravestone. She picked up the binoculars and fixed them on the spot. Her heart leapt. Yes, it was M all right. He'd come at last. Her hands trembled, causing the long, lanky form in the glass to waver as it dropped to the ground to sit crosslegged by the stone. He carried two large shrubs, their roots bound in burlap. He had a pack on his back and one in front as well. That was strange. He emptied the front pack and there in M's hands, like an offering to Buster, lay a newborn baby.

Running, ducking low as she ran, she headed for the back of Buster's knoll, hitting the ground to crawl up the back of it, squirming through low chaparrel, to the sheltering clump of oak. She heard the baby cry, then stop crying. She peeked around to see M giving it a bottle. God!

"Well, Buster," Masef said. "Here's your little grandchild, Buster the Second. Of course, I had to right away bring him to see you. He's only six weeks old. There was a little trouble about my leaving. Most mother's can't dig the idea of their baby being taken away to meet a gravestone so soon after being born.

Luckily, or sorrowfully, Cecile isn't that devoted a mother. She wouldn't even nurse him. Isn't that sad?

"To tell the truth, Buster the Second may not be my baby. But that doesn't matter. I feel such a love for him, more than I ever did for anyone but you. Well, and Sunny too, and Masefield and Laurie. And Amy who I've wronged so horribly.

"But this love is so uncomplicated. He's just a beginning person, can't see me yet or know who I am. Already I'm so scared of something happening to him. But fear of losing a person is the worst reason in the world not to love. We're all going to lose each other. That's what life is. You can't blame a person for dying. They die when they have to, for one reason or another. They die or go away or stop loving you. I shouldn't have blamed Sunny for not loving you enough. Look at me. Look at all the people I haven't loved enough. It's so easy to judge when you're young. Then you live along a little and see how hard it all is.

"But I have to tell you that Cecile doesn't seem to love this baby—probably because of all the trouble she's been through. But it scares me. Maybe that's why I love the little guy so much because I can't think of anything sadder than a newborn baby not being loved by his mother, not being nursed. I don't understand women, Buster. A father, if he could nurse, would never not do it."

Masef took a blanket from his backpack and wrapped the baby into a tight cocoon, putting him safely by the stone while he set about cleaning up the gravesite, clearing debris from beneath the trees, weeding around the shrubs, all the while chatting to Buster, sometimes simply humming happily, or just being quiet as he beautified the resting place of the friend he'd lost when he was four.

Laurie crept away, back to camp. She waited about an hour, giving Masef his private time with the grave, then saddled her horse, and came riding by just as he was planting the new bushes he'd brought—a wild azalea and a huckleberry.

He greeted her gladly but with astonishment. "Laurie, how could you possibly have known I'd be here today?"

She dismounted. "I have to admit I've been watching for you. Everyone's been worried about your long absence and Masefield has been unable to find you. Oh, M, how beautiful he is." She leaned over the baby not feigning surprise, but truly surprised and affected by the sweet, lovely face in the swaddling clothes, the jewel-like features, the translucent skin, the enchanting newness. The baby, at the sound of her voice, opened wondering eyes. M's child. How she longed to put him to her own breast to make up for the ones denied him. Oh, to be a mother to M's child.

"This is Buster the Second," he said proudly. "It sort of sounds like a name out of the *Icelandic Sagas,* doesn't it?" He laughed. "I'm so happy, Laurie. I was just telling Buster that I finally found out what I want to be in life—a father."

"M, I've got to talk to you. Are you finished here?"

He looked around, pleased with his work, but loath to go. "I guess so. It looks pretty nice, doesn't it?"

"Yes."

They walked over to her camp, the horse following. She brewed some coffee. They drank and talked. The whole time, Masef held the baby.

Months ago, at the start of her stakeout, Laurie had

prepared a long speech about the situation—the crime. As time passed, she forgot it, almost forgot the reason for her camping as the camping became a reason of its own.

So now she simply said, "We think Cecile, herself, might have killed Baby." She told him about the recreation of Baby's death. He listened with no particular expression. "We think she would have killed Boy, too, if you and Amy hadn't got there."

He was quiet. Laurie didn't know what she'd expected, but it was pretty powerful news. Maybe he didn't need to tear his hair and beat his breast, but he ought to at least look interested.

"How's Amy?" he asked, as if that was the important part, the main text of her news.

Laurie thought back to the evening on the porch. Although she'd expected Boy to be the maimed one, she'd hardly recognized Amy, her stricken white face, her forlorn presence. She looked like a shut-in.

She shrugged off the images. That wasn't the point.

"M, listen to me. The woman you're with is bad. Killer bad. You've got to leave her."

M looked pained. "Laurie. You've always been so jealous. So possessive. You're shackled by it and you try to shackle me. You've got to let me live my life."

"But I'm not jealous this time!" she protested, feeling afraid that he wouldn't believe her. "This hasn't to do with jealousy!"

She'd left off her whole life to come and warn him, save him.

M shook his head sadly, as if she were a hopeless case.

"If you don't believe me," she said intensely, trying to burn the words through his misapprehension, "talk to Masefield. You'll believe him."

"He didn't like Cecile from the start."

Laurie got mad at what she considered to be his stupidness, his locked mind. "With good reason as it turns out. She destroyed Boy and Amy. Now she'll destroy you if you go back."

"Laurie, the poor woman has been through so much. I could never desert her. And I couldn't leave baby Buster. Or take him away from his own mother."

"You've taken him away already. Keep on going," she pleaded. "Take off. You have before."

"You're asking the impossible of me. I'm sorry, but I don't trust you. You're a brave woman—but irrational."

Laurie seized on the word brave and ignored the rest, didn't even hear the word woman or what followed.

You're a brave, he said, meaning an Indian warrior, meaning a person of splendid courage. She felt her bosom swell as with milk at the cry of a child. She was a brave and would travel this war path to the end, splendidly, courageously, unmoved by M's wrongheaded mewlings about "poor Cecile."

As a brave, she despised her jealousy of the past, her "clinging" as Ito described it, saw now how it did diminish her, did shackle her. But even at this moment of truth, this slaying of the green-eyed monster, she said, "You don't love Cecile!" uttering the immortal cry of the jealous woman, the most jealoussounding words of all.

"I do love her. I pity her."

"Who wants to be pitied? No one normal. Pity is the currency she deals in. To cleave men to her. Erotic pity. Those were Masefield's words."

"I pity you, too, Laurie."

A knife to the heart.

"Now we've got to go, Buster and I. I promised I'd be home by tonight."

"Will you give me your address?"

He hesitated. "I'll send it to Masefield," he said gently—as if any kindness of tone could make distrust sound better. "Goodbye, Laurie."

She wanted to yell, Don't leave Buster alone with her! Would that sound jealous? Yes. Everything she said would. He didn't know she'd changed, that fifteen minutes ago, or during the last two months, she'd changed from a squaw to a brave and this freed her so that for the first time in her life she didn't care how he felt about her; she just cared about him.

He didn't seem to have a car with him. There weren't buses. He'd probably hitched. So he couldn't have come from that far away. Probably he was hiding out up the coast where it was wild. Not in a city. And she didn't think he'd be inland. She bet he was in some remote coastal village in Mendocino County, somewhere like that. However, before leaving Pt. Reyes, he'd definitely go by and see Sunny. He said he had to be back tonight. It was after noon . . .

He was almost out of earshot now.

"Don't leave Buster alone with her!" she shouted.

He turned and called to her with an instruction of his own, "Don't follow me."

Laurie stood still and watched him go, his long, lean frame walking differently than previously, as if the wee weight of the babe had centered him. Masef, no longer a flighty boy, but a man striding purposely away into the landscape.

She watched him almost out of sight, not batting an eye. Then she followed him.

TWENTY

A baby. I put down the phone (which I'd run to). Buster the Second. I stood stock still, dazed by the news, disoriented. A Baby.

"Boy, you ran to the phone!" Amy said, coming into the study. "Do you know that you ran to the phone?" She looked at me. "What's the matter? You're white as a ghost."

"Amy. That was Laurie. She's seen Masef." Now she turned white. "He's okay," I said quickly. I hugged her. We hugged each other hard with happiness and relief and Amy babbled away so that I couldn't say the next thing yet, about the baby. Then finally, "Amy, he had a baby with him."

"A baby?"

"Yes. Newborn. It could be mine, or his. Amy, I could be a father. I think I am. I think I'm a father, Amy. Imagine. A little boy. His name is Buster."

"Buster."

We stood there repeating the news over and over, coming to grips with it. "Baby." "Buster." It was so enormous. We were clutching each other's hands. Outside, it was raining persistently and although it was only four o'clock it seemed like night. Amy had just set a fire in the living room fireplace and we walked over to it releasing our hands to stretch them out to the heat.

"He came to Buster's grave?" Amy asked. "Was that where she saw them?"

"Yes."

"Laurie talked to him?"

Poor Amy was waiting for me to give her news of his homecoming.

"He didn't believe her about Cecile, Amy. He thought Laurie was just being obsessively jealous, as usual."

"We should have thought of that," Amy said woefully. "Damn!"

"He said he wouldn't leave Cecile. He wouldn't tell Laurie where he lived, but she followed him. Up near the Oregon border, a town called Weed. They have a little house there."

They have a little house there. The words smote Amy. It sounded so settled, so cozy and loving. It sounded way better than a big house . . . certainly better than a little cottage with a hole in it.

"He didn't believe about Cecile maybe murdering Baby?" Amy asked.

After her initial joy at his being alive and well with a baby named Buster, she felt rapid deflation as the knowledge seeped in that he wasn't coming home, that he was in a little house.

She looked around her own house in its state of constant readiness: the fresh flowers in fresh water, his favorite books on the coffee table, a Segovia tape in the stereo. Even the lilies of the pond awaited further hand wrestling contests, peering pinkly from the dark waters of his or her imminent defeat. He'd been gone almost ten months.

"At least Masef is warned about her," she said weakly, trying to see the good.

"Yes, but what about the baby? He could be mine

even though he tried to claim him by calling him
Buster. Amy, I'm going to go up there and try to get
him away."

"But how?"

"If I'm the father, I have as much right to him as
she does."

"But what if Masef thinks he's the father?"

"He couldn't be. The timing isn't right. Unless it
was premature."

She said painfully, "The timing could be right if
they were lovers from the start. I think they were
lovers the whole time she was here. We never had sex
together after she came. No, not once."

The last time was the day he got home. He'd carried her into the little cottage like a bride, bumping
his head on the lintel. They'd undressed very slowly.
He'd exclaimed at her hard-won tan. He started telling her about a movie he'd seen, a western, and continued telling her about it, acting out the different
parts, while he brought her to orgasm. It had been
fun. He held off his own orgasm until the shootout at
the end, slamming into her as the shots rang out, letting loose his death (or victory) howl. It had been
wonderful. Then they'd wrapped their arms around
each other and slept.

"Amy, listen to me. Stop dreaming. I'm going to
plead with him to let me take Buster. Even if she
didn't kill Baby, she was a terrible mother. He'll get
no attention, no love. She will neglect him, maybe
abuse him."

"But, Boy, think! I hate to remind you, but you
have to remember that Masef believes you, not Cecile, were the cause of Baby's death, and therefore he
won't dream of relinquishing Buster to your care.
He'll think you're the neglectful one. It will always

just be our word against hers. We'll never have proof. And she's the one he loves. She's the one he's with, not us."

Helplessly she pictured the "little house"—painted blue, she imagined, with pink roses clambering over it, birds fluttering around, singing away, a silvery brook running through the yard—a perfect little dream cottage.

"I'm going," I said.

"Masefield should be the one to go. Masef will believe him. Or Ito. Why not get Ito to go?"

"I'm going. This is my baby and I've got to take responsibility."

I copied the address Laurie had given me and left the original with Amy. "Here." I put it in her hand, kissed her, grabbed my trench coat and ran through the rain to the car at the end of the driveway. I ran, not involuntarily, but meaning to.

TWENTY-ONE

When Masef and Buster the Second returned to Weed from their whirlwind visit to Inverness, it was 10:00 P.M.

Masef paused before entering the house, looking toward Mount Shasta which was erased by the night. He tried to catch its outline by the absence of stars, the negative space, but he couldn't. He stood for a while, looking at the night sky, murmuring to Buster about the different contellations, even though the baby slept.

"There's Orion, my favorite. There's the Big Teddy Bear. And the Big Dipper. It's full of beer for me and the Little Dipper has warm milk and honey for you. I hate to tell you, but those millions of stars above us are just one galaxy. There's others. Millions more. It makes you feel damned unimportant. It's supposed to. Still, I think you're the most important baby in this galaxy."

The setting of the house, on a road above the railroad tracks, across from a supermarket and next to an automotive parts store, was somber—as was the whole town.

At first it had been a hideout from which they meant to move, but, with Cecile being ill with her pregnancy and depressed by Baby's "murder" as she called it, inertia set in. They stayed in Weed.

Since it was a factory town, Masef found work in the peeler plant where they made veneer. In the summer and fall he ardently pursued the wily trout (sometimes the salmon)—the best fly fishing of his life. By late November, he geared up for cross-country skiing, but by then more and more time had to be given to Cecile and to Buster. Presently he had no job, no sport, and no travel except for his grueling twelve-hour hitch today.

So he paused before entering, feeling no joy at his return, keenly aware of the somber setting, the bleak house, the downhearted woman within. He even felt despair, a feeling his happy nature was reluctant to acknowledge.

It's just three wooden steps and a door, he thought, *but I feel like I'm entering a steel trap, that a huge porcullis will come clanging down behind me once I step inside. Then chains will fall on me from the ceiling, irons will sidle from the walls to clamp my appendages. But I have to go in. I'm out of diapers.*

When he walked in, Cecile was sitting in the living room which, along with the kitchen, bedroom, and an alcove they'd fixed up for Buster, made up the whole house. She sprawled on the couch in front of the woodstove which was not lit, wearing a dingy kimono. By the light of a dim lamp, Masef saw she was cleaning her gun, a not uncommon sight. She was intent on her task and did not greet either of them, neither man nor babe, did not look up from her work of swabbing out the barrel with a brush.

Masef blanched at the scene before him. He took Buster to the alcove, put him down in the bassinet, and pulled the curtain across the space. Returning to the living room, he shucked off his parka and sweater, then sat by Cecile on the couch. "Well, I'm back when I said I would be."

"Yes." She still didn't look at him. "So I see. You get to find me alive. If you didn't return, I was going to shoot myself. I thought you had taken the baby and gone forever."

He put the gun on the table and took her hands in his. "Why did you think that?"

Her blond hair, which had grown long during her pregnancy, was loose around her face. She looked like a child. She fixed him with her large liquid eyes, which for some reason looked brown to him instead of blue. "You love the baby more than me."

"I love you both. Please call him Buster. He has a name."

"What if you had found me dead?"

"I would be sad as hell." Masef was trying to keep the conversation light, but it was rough going.

"Would you kill yourself?"

"No," he said honestly, giving up on the lightness.

"Boy's mother killed herself after she lost his father," she said dreamily. "I thought that was so wonderful. It was partly what drew me to Boy. I thought he would love me that passionately. But no." Now her voice was dry and bitter. "He loved his running more. Much more."

"He's a great runner. You have to be single-minded to be that great," Masef defended him. Was, he amended silently, was a great runner. "Shall I make a fire?"

"Masef, darling. Promise me you won't ever leave me."

"I'm not going to leave you, Cecile."

"Then why do you say you won't die with me?"

"Die with you? The idea is to live with you."

"Die if I die," she insisted. "Not leave me on my own in the afterlife."

"There isn't an afterlife. This is it. Live it with all your might." He started to make a fire, placing the paper, sticks, and logs with careful absorption. Then he lit it and watched its combustion with satisfaction. Sitting back down beside her, he treasured the moment of silence because he knew she wasn't through —she hadn't cried yet.

"I want to make a pact, that if one of us dies, the other will, too. Like Boy's parents."

"No. It's not fair to orphan a kid. It's mean and selfish." He thought about how Buster the First had died for love of Sunny, leaving him forever. Why did death seem to enoble love, when it only left a little kid by himself?

Maybe because without death, love died of itself. Love wore out. He certainly was finding this conversation wearing. Maybe she was in one of those postpartum depressions the doctor alerted him about (to add on to her prepartum one). He should be sympathetic.

But it was very rough going. The fire helped a little. The flames were so pretty. And in a minute he'd have a beer. There were compensations. Digging deep, he rousted out some kind words.

"Cecile, honey, you're just in a down mood because I went off and left you for the day and it's been a long day. I love you. I'm not going to leave you. All this talk of death and suicide isn't healthy. Let's create a good life for Buster so he'll grow up strong and kind."

He stood up, scooping away the gun and the cleaning kit. "Anything to eat around here? More importantly, any beer?"

As if she hadn't heard a word he'd spoken, Cecile grabbed hold of his arm and said intensely, "Promise me you'll kill yourself if I die."

Masef sighed. Sometimes it was just easier to lie. "I promise," he said.

She smiled. She beamed. She looked so happy he was glad he'd caved in. When a woman got unreasonable, it was the best thing. It saved a lot of grief. And it had its rewards. He could have a beer with a happy heart. But she had another reward in mind for she pulled him down and kissed his eyes, nose, ears, mouth, her tongue touching his tear ducts, his nostrils, his earholes. His body caught fire. It had been a long time.

Expertly, she undid his belt and fly to put her tongue where he liked it best. This was a wonderful reward, indeed. He gave himself over to the pleasure. Maybe it wasn't worth dying for, but it was certainly worth *saying* you'd die. This was positive reinforcement for his coming around to being negative. Compensation city. He realized that enough time had gone by since Buster's birth that they could have full sex again. That would make things better between them. Feeling the strength of her cheeks and tongue, the pull of her throat, all thoughts were stilled. There was only sensation. And fire.

When they were finished and he was drowsing happily, Cecile's head on his stomach, he stroking her silvery blonde hair, Buster began to cry. Masef tensed and his caressing hand froze. Cecile did not move. His instinct was to leap up and see to him, but another instinct warned him not to do so and incur her wrath thereby. He sensed she would view any action on his part as their own tender time despoiled.

But it wrung his heart hearing the vulnerable, beseeching wail. Gently as all hell, carefully finding just the right loving tone, he asked, "Do you want me to go or shall you?"

"Go where?"

Masef simply did not know what to do with this response.

Forcing tenderness into his touch, he carefully set her aside and pushed himself up from the couch. While doing so, his hand hit something hard. It was a tape recorder. "What's this?" he joked. "Were you recording my moans?"

"No. That was to leave my farewell message with. My suicide note. I've never been any good at writing." She smiled. "See to the baby, will you honey?"

TWENTY-TWO

"He's in Weed, California," Laurie told Masefield by telephone after she'd recounted her unsuccessful meeting with Masef in Inverness. "So am I. I followed him here. It's a dreary little company town dominated, not so much by Mt. Shasta, as by the factory, which has to be the biggest wooden building in the world. You could put all the little houses of the town inside and still have room for the Pentagon. Why Weed? is all I keep asking myself. Why Weed?"

"Hat Creek and Fall River," Masefield answered.

"What? Who?"

"It's some of the world's best trout fishing."

"M fishes?"

"Passionately."

"I didn't know," Laurie said tonelessly. "Here I believe I know him better than anyone . . ."

"Fly fishermen only talk about it to each other. We recognize each other at fifty paces—by the set of the shoulders, the gentle hands. Bless you, Laurie, I'm on my way."

"It's a white house on Weed Boulevard, which is motel and gas station row so you can get a room practically next door. I'm camping out and freezing my ass off. Don't tell him I'm here. He said not to follow him. See ya."

Masefield called Ito with the news, then flew to San Francisco where, after a restless night's sleep, his friend joined him in his hotel room for breakfast.

"I may have to kill this woman, Ito. I tell you that as a priest. It is between the two of us."

Ito poured himself some coffee. He'd been trying to quit the stuff to no avail. There were too many things in life to quit. You end up with no life left. *It's all an illusion anyhow,* he told himself. *Even coffee is an illusion. Certainly giving it up is.*

One thing he had quit successfully, however, was killing. Since Vietnam, except for the year of his mad passion for Mer, who was now his wife, he'd led a gentle life, trying to awaken himself and others, trying to look after them. Right now, he tried to look after Masefield.

He gave him his most compassionate look, which Masefield ignored.

Ito has two main expressions, Masefield said to himself. Dumb and compassionate. Both of which, especially when I am on a mission, which I conceive this trip to Weed to be, I find completely exasperating. But I'll forbear. Because I need him.

Ito read his mind, lowered his eyes, drank coffee.

"Laurie told me Masef refuses to leave Cecile," Masefield explained. "He didn't believe Laurie's information, thought it was jealousy talking. Therefore it's up to me to do something."

"You are always . . ." (Ito tried not to say interfering) ". . . arranging Masef's life. I wonder how he will manage when you are dead."

Masefield sent his laser glance over to the big Samoan and his easygoing voice had an edge to it when he said, "Maybe Masef can look after himself. But my six-week-old grandson can't."

"Ah, yes, little baby Buster the Second." Ito smiled. "Don't you think Masef will see to his safety? You said Laurie described him as loving the infant very much."

"Masef loves everybody very much, including the murderer he lives with." Masefield paused, cracked open his egg, ate toast. He continued coolly. "You felt remorse that you hadn't warned him about Cecile."

"That's right, I did say that—out of love and grief. But I would have been wrong to interfere, to let my emotions unbalance me to that extent."

"Wrong to have saved Boy from all that he's been through? Come on, Ito."

"We don't like to see our loved ones suffer, but maybe Boy will be a better man for all this. Things don't entirely *happen* to us. We, in part, cause them to happen."

"Okay, so Boy has a chance to grow and learn. No pain, no gain. However," he pointed a finger at Ito, "Baby doesn't have a chance because Baby is dead as a doornail."

"True," Ito granted him. Now he wore his dumb expression, but it was not impenetrably so. "How sure are we that Cecile intentionally murdered her child or her husband, or tried to murder Boy?"

"We aren't sure. We only have our gut feelings. Mine have become conviction. I'm convinced by the re-creation Amy and Boy performed of the accident." Masefield finished his breakfast, got up and put on a shoulder holster over his crisp white shirt. He holstered his Walther and pulled on a tweed jacket. "I've always had trouble killing women. Its almost been the death of me a couple of times."

"You are a man who has to know, has to be sure," Ito reminded him.

"That's why I want you to come with me, Ito. To look into her heart."

"And finger her? Be an accessory? I don't murder anymore. You know that. I'm trying to be a Buddha."

"You have to calculate the benefit, Ito."

Ito said nothing, now looking impenetrably dumb, too dumb to calculate. It was an enviable affect, which his admirers tried and failed to master. Ito could even make his eyes look closed when they were open.

Even Masefield, who'd known Ito for a score of years, was impressed into feeling he was dealing with a Neanderthal.

He raised his voice as if that were the case, as if Neanderthals were hard of hearing. "The Bodhisattva says he will do wrong to stop wrongdoing," Masefield repeated what Ito had once told him. "He will kill to stop killing. As an exception. He calls it 'doing surgery, not violence.' You remove the one killer to stop many killings. Is this true?"

"This is true," Ito granted.

"Ito, it is on the strength of this belief that I am asking you to come with me to Weed. I'm asking you to help me. Will you?"

The big Samoan sighed, rose to his feet. "Yes."

Masefield flashed one of his rare smiles . . . he had surprisingly beautiful teeth. Feeling a relief comparable to being let off the rack (a relief he'd actually experienced in his spying days). "Thanks, old buddy. I'm damned grateful. It's always good to get a second opinion before doing surgery."

"I'm hoping to look into her heart and find it undefiled." Ito realized he was sounding sententious and hated himself. It was so hard to stay on the path without coming across as a prick.

"I have us a plane to Klamath Falls and a fast Italian car at the airport. Let's go."

"It's been ten months. What's the big hurry now?"

"Even if Masef didn't pass on our suspicions to Cecile, I feel like the cat's out of the bag, Ito. Claws out. I'm scared."

Ito was scared, too.

Maybe that's why I sound so self-righteous, he told himself forgivingly, *because I'm scared.*

TWENTY-THREE

Amy also joined the exodus to Weed. After Boy dashed out of the house, she spent an hour in front of the hearth, watching fire in the way she watched rain, letting her mind roam. Where it roamed was to Masef and Baby Buster and the uselessness of Boy's errand. Then it roamed home again, feeling the emptiness all about her—the house that was all fixed up for Masef's return, now his non-return.

She missed him so much. She felt so lonely. And yet it had been a loss she couldn't even talk about because Boy's trouble was so much more gigantic, it put hers in the shade. She almost felt embarassed to be so sad, so devastated.

What if, she thought, Masef doesn't know how to come home? What if he thinks I don't want him or can't forgive him for abandoning us? Maybe he doesn't know I still love him and that there's a light in the window. It could be, could well be, that he isn't happy with Cecile and wants to come home but doesn't know how. Maybe I should go to Weed and invite him home.

She felt she'd been good just letting him be. But then she'd let him be Cecile's. Was that good? She'd been passive. She'd let that woman come into her and Boy's life and completely ruin it, especially Boy's, and done nothing.

She hadn't known where Masef was. Or known for sure that he was with Cecile. So it made some sense to keep on waiting and hoping. Now she had the address in her hand where Boy had thrust it as he kissed her goodbye.

Amy didn't consciously make a decision to go to Weed to invite Masef home, but when she got up the next morning she started preparing to go, to close the house, pack a few things, and go.

It occurred to her that she didn't care about coming home again herself if he wouldn't come with her. Or if she knew for certain he wouldn't be coming eventually. She would gladly return to wait for him, but if he was not coming that was just stupid. She might as well find out what the deal was and take it from there. Get a life, she told herself.

She shut the door and bolted across the rain puddles to throw her bag into the car her mother had driven to her suicide because life without her husband was insupportable.

My pain is supportable, Amy told herself, as she adjusted the rearviews and started the engine and the wipers. *But maybe that's because I have hope. Mom had no hope of his return. Now I'm going to maybe get rid of the hope in Weed. Still, it's the best thing. No sense in my dragging around with a supportable pain when maybe I can get rid of it—or make it worse.*

She took off down the driveway in a spray of gravel and turned north. She asked herself if she was at all afraid of encountering Cecile and answered no. But there was a good chance of running into Laurie and she still admitted to having a fear of her. The fact that the woman had camped over three months in one spot in order to find Masef bespoke a diligence and fortitude that only increased her awe. Here was not a

passive woman. And the fact that Amy was only following the trail Laurie had blazed didn't show any
particular courage, fortitude, or diligence on her part.
Except it was something to be leaving home and town
for the first time in almost a year.

Amy felt good about herself and gave herself
credit: *I know how brave I'm being to go to faraway Weed
even though it only looks ordinary on the outside, looks like
I'm just tagging along.*

As she hit highway 101 North, she lightened up to
where she found herself smiling, even joking. *I'm not
only leaving home, I'm forsaking my post, she thought. I'm
leaving the town all vulnerable with no one to watch the
rain. Maybe I should have appointed somebody?*

*I wonder where the heck Weed is? I better stop for a map.
And some gas. And money. There's more to leaving home
than shutting the door and leaping puddles.*

Five hours later, on I5, Amy came across Boy's
Volvo at the side of the road. She pulled over and
checked it out to see if Boy was there, but there was
no sign of him. Of course, there wouldn't be. He was
twelve hours ahead of her and must now be well en-
sconced in Weed, must have talked to Masef and Cecile, seen the baby. What a hard thing he was doing.
She, too. Together, maybe they would prevail. Orphans united!

TWENTY-FOUR

Motoring through the storm-streaked night, the Volvo had contracted the automotive disease called "a funny noise." The noise became more gravely funny as the miles wheeled by, the car developing symptoms of spiritlessness and reluctance, finally leading to acute nonacceleration. It was two in the morning, the rain still pelting down. I crawled into the backseat and slept.

I awoke to a watery dawn, but the rain was little more than a mist now and the air was fairly warm. The highway was empty of cars but full of the volcano which, because it is a solitary peak rising from a plain of four thousand to a height of fifteen thousand, filled the sky pretty handily, with white snow above timberline, green firs and pines below.

I stood out, trying to hitch, with no luck. No one seemed to get up early to go to work around here; probably why Masef had chosen the area.

I began to feel wet and cold. I opened the trunk to see what extra clothes I had in there since I generally threw stuff in rather than pack when I went from Berkeley to home. What I saw was a pair of sweats from my running days—worn, bleached, wrinkled, but thick and dry. There were about three pairs of running shoes, too, buried under a blanket that I could happily have used in the night.

I changed from my jeans and wet loafers into my sweats and running shoes, stepped out on the highway and didn't put out my thumb.

Instead, I started to jog.

I jogged along the side of the highway, going slow and easy. The sun rose, the air cleared, puffy saffron clouds littered the sky, the volcano's snowy heights suffused with rose. Every so often a car passed, tires hissing on the wet macadam but now my thumb was in, just part of my hand moving with the rhythm of my stride.

I was running. It was wonderful. Absolutely wonderful. The air was great, going in and out of my lungs in the way it does only when you run, whereby you are *aware* that you're breathing. You hear and feel yourself breathing, but it is easy, not agitated.

Yes. I was breathing the good air. I was happy. I forgot everything except that I was running. I kept on, bypassing the towns, heading for Weed. I'd send someone for the car later. I would run to Weed. Why not? What was the hurry? I felt I could run forever, that I could run up Mount Shasta, over the snowfields and hot rocks, dodging the fumeroles, then trot on down the other side. Just keep on going.

I kept on, not running fast, just putting in the miles, putting them away. It was up hill almost the whole time. I was running at altitude, up a butte, as I realized when I saw a sign saying, Black Butte Summit, 3,912. Then it was a gentle descent to Weed, where I arrived after almost four hours of putting one foot in front of the other.

I went into a place called the Ranch Restaurant and wolfed down a stack of flapjacks with a gallon of water and juices and coffee—a celebratory feast. I sat there blithely eating and drinking for about an hour, checking out the *Weed Press* which someone had left at the table.

It seemed like a nice little town. The big news was a fire that wiped out a family's possessions and everyone chipped in with a new place to live and plenty of clothes and furniture and toys for the kids. There were articles on environmental concerns regarding the "Sacred Mountain" and, equally important, how the high school basketball team was doing. Pictures of brides and grooms that city papers don't go in for any more, took up one whole page. The Shasta Players putting on Brigadoon took up another. Elsewhere, a man had fired a rifle at his brother (hadn't hit him) and was booked for disturbing the peace and challenging to fight—both counts of which could have put me, Amy, Masefield and Ito in jail after our free-for-all on the lawn.

When I stood up, I could hardly walk. My whole body went into a spasm. The thing was I didn't have any running muscles to do all that running with. I was just running on memory, on the running memory locked into my nervous system. The body can do things like that. But it's hard on the muscles that aren't there anymore. I smiled, thinking, now they know where they are and having relocated themselves, can begin to grow and define themselves. This is just the beginning! Boy Freeling's coming back. Look out world.

I hobbled and limped my way out of the cafe and looked for Masef's place. It turned out to be only a few doors down the road.

TWENTY-FIVE

I paused before the door. What was I feeling? On a wave of emotion from learning about the baby, I'd come pell mell to Weed without considering how it was going to be to see Cecile again. But apparently I still wished to waive any emotional examination because I simply lifted my hand and knocked.

"I'm looking for Masef Scott," I said to the woman who answered.

"Don't you recognize me?" She seemed pleased—not so much to see me as the fact that I didn't know her.

"Cecile?" I was surprised and shaken. Hearing her voice, I could see it was her. But her hair was longer and lighter. She was heavier.

"Your eyes are brown." I just lit on one thing aloud. Even the shape of her brows were different.

"Lenses," she said.

"But why?"

"I like changing my looks. It gives me a new lease on life, which I severely need right now. Come in. It's cold." She shut the door. I followed her to the stove like I was on a leash, feeling the old pull of her attraction.

Funny that I should be the surprised one, not her. My sudden appearance seemed to mean nothing to her. But I remembered she was always a woman who had herself in hand, who chose her emotions, didn't let emotions claim her. For all I knew, she could be wild with dismay.

I was upset. My heart was beating hard.

"Masef doesn't notice," she complained, still talking about herself. "He never says anything about my appearance. I suppose you've come to see the baby. Masef told me he'd seen his mother, so I guess everybody knows by now."

"I do want to see the baby. Is he my baby, Cecile?" I'd meant to lead up to this question, but I blurted it out.

She shrugged. "I have no idea."

"I think he must be."

"So what if he were?"

"I would want to be a father to him. I *do* want to be."

She said nothing, only sat down on the couch and looked at me. She was wearing a silk kimono colored with cranes and flowers. It seemed so odd to see her in this pitiful and shabby little house. She had luxuriated in my house, which had suited her. This didn't.

Maybe the new lease on life she needed included a change of locale.

Incredibly I heard my voice say, "I've had a dream that we would be together again, with our own baby to love." I was still blurting, as if my racing heart was accelerating my plans, pushing unreasonable words from my mouth. But it was true. I had had that dream, had sustained it against all odds.

"I know you wanted your *own* baby," she said, her voice suddenly turning hard as nails. "That's why you killed my baby, because he was some other man's."

I sat down, giving a gasp of pain from both my

muscles and her words. "It was an accident." I defended myself. I was on the defense, I who had come armed with belief in myself.

"You killed Baby. Now you dare to want me back."

"I didn't kill her, Cecile. You know that I didn't."

"How do I know?"

"Baby couldn't have got to the car on her own. She couldn't crawl."

"Oh, yes, she could crawl," she said. "Because you taught her to."

"What?" The room seemed to rock.

"Don't you remember that day on the lawn when you showed her how to crawl?"

"But, Cecile . . ."

"You set it up to look like an accident. But you taught her to crawl. Then you got her fascinated with the garage door opening."

She was saying all this with complete conviction. She was turning the little interest I'd shown in Baby into an accusation, into facts against me.

"Now you dare to ask me to come back to you. With my new baby. You must be mad. Stark raving mad."

I wasn't mad, but I was stupid to have proceeded the way I did. Maybe the running had unhinged me.

"Where is the baby?" I looked around.

"With Masef. At the laundry. He should be back any minute."

I could see she meant me to take this as a warning to leave.

"I'm staying," I said. "I want to see him."

She shrugged and picked up a magazine as if I were no longer there as far as she was concerned. Pale sunlight came through the window, but only augmented the general cheerlessness.

We remained in silence. Having spouted out all my stupid words, there was nothing left to say.

After a while, Masef arrived. He greeted me in a friendly way and seemed to look at me with pity. Afterward, I realized it was because I was so crippled from my long marathon of the morning. He thought that was the way I normally moved, that the great runner now shuffled around barely getting from one chair to the next.

When he took Buster out of the bodypack and showed me him, I was dazzled.

Cecile said the worst thing she could under the circumstances. "Imagine this, Masef, Boy has come to beg me to return home with him. He wants me back. Me and the baby."

Now he would never believe what Laurie had told him, since my own actions completely contradicted her words. If I really believed Cecile to be a murderer, why would I ask her back?

Because I didn't believe it. It was too intolerable to think she'd done it. I couldn't learn to believe she'd purposely kill Baby.

I hadn't in the least *begged* her to come back, had only mentioned the dream. Still, it was true that being with her again made me want to obliterate the whole thing and start fresh with my own baby. And, yes, with her, too. I must still love her.

So I told Masef, "I want to be a father to the baby."

"Buster's my baby," he said. He hugged Buster close as I reached for him.

"I'm sure he's mine," I said. "The time elapsed is proof enough."

Masef turned away.

"Won't you let me hold him?"

"No," he said firmly. Then, again, he looked at me pityingly. "I'm sorry, Boy. I know you've been through hell. And I'm willing to believe it was an accident. But it's no good, your coming here. I will never let you have Buster."

Cecile seemed to be enjoying the scene. "Why don't you cut him in half?"

Masef and I locked eyes, shocked.

Masef's reaction was to pass me the baby after all.

He was so tiny and fragile. He seemed like such a good little guy. He looked like me, I thought, but then Masef and I were cousins and there was a family resemblance.

"Poor Masef," Cecile crooned. "What if I said Buster was Boy's? What if I said he could take him? What would you do then? Would you go with the baby? Or would you stay with me?"

So the baby had come between them in the same way that my running had come between us. "Poor Masef" was right. My heart went out to him. And yet, what she said gave me hope. I could play on that to get the baby away.

"I'm not leaving here without the baby," I said.

TWENTY-SIX

There was not a fast Italian car waiting for Masefield and Ito at the Yreka Airport. Siskiyou County didn't go in for that sort of thing—more like pickup trucks with gun racks—so he had to settle for a lowly Chevy, ill-running to boot, arriving a half hour later, as opposed to waiting meekly for them. Masefield's consummate connections didn't reach to California's northern mountains.

He took the inefficiency in stride. Masefield took everything in stride, never wasted wrath. Ito was not as unflappable as Masefield, no one was, but he could zen his way through most situations.

When the Chevy finally did arrive and Masefield drove it a hundred yards in a cloud of pestilential exhaust, he simply got out and took the pilot's own car—a pilot would have a car that ran well—promising to have it back by evening for the flight home. Such was Masefield's impressiveness that the pilot was honored to have his car so summarily commandeered.

They drove to Weed and, after getting the lay of the land, parked a few blocks from Masef's house. Masefield shunned parking in front of any place he was going to enter. While walking along, rounding a corner, they ran into me and Masef and Baby Buster the Second.

"Dad!" Masef's first reaction was, as usual, joy at seeing his father, seconded only by mine at seeing Ito, and there were hugs and exclamations all around and much showing and handing around of Buster. "There he is," said Ito admiringly and yearningly. "Still blessed with his beautiful unborn Buddha mind that we are all trying to get back to after having ours hopelessly sullied by knowledge. Teach me, Buster, teach me."

"Dad, why are you here?" Masef asked.

"I've come to see you, of course, and meet my grandson. Also, I want to talk to Cecile."

"Dad, you are not to accuse her," Masef spoke imperatively. He wasn't kidding. Masefield looked (for him) surprised and (for him) slightly at a loss. "You are not to say anything to distress her." Masef continued to give his father orders. "She is still weak from the pregnancy and birth. She's physically and emotionally frail. She suffers a lot."

He'd learned that line from Cecile herself, I thought grimly, remembering all the times she'd talked about her "suffering." But she had suffered, I reminded myself. She had. But so had Amy and I. So had everyone.

"Don't worry," Masefield told him, not in a flip way but in a way that honored his son's feelings.

"I do worry. I know it has been awful for Boy," he gestured at the pitiable wreck he perceived to be me, "and for Amy . . . how is Amy?"

No one answered. It was as if deep down everyone thought Amy was the most hurt but couldn't give words to it, just as she couldn't herself. She was so loving and giving. Was I loving? I asked myself. Did I love? Or did I just want?

Masef continued ". . . but Boy himself obviously

doesn't believe in this crap about Cecile or he wouldn't have asked her to come back to him."

At this, I turned all colors. Ito and Masefield looked my way, but did not betray the astonishment they must have felt, did not fall down on the ground and foam at the mouth. I wanted to explain that I'd only said I'd had a dream of getting back together and Cecile had blown it up to a big on-the-knees begging of her to return. But I couldn't protest without looking more the fool. I just shrugged helplessly.

"We're only going by to pay our respects," Masefield said calmly. Then I knew that Masefield wanted Ito to meet her and look into her heart. It made my own heart start to beat erratically. All would be revealed. God, he'd brought Ito all the hell the way up here to look into her heart. And Ito had come!

Masefield wasn't kidding, either.

Then something else occurred to me.

"Ito could tell us who the father is," I said to Masef, trying to keep the excitement from my voice. "You or me. He'd know. He probably already knows. He's a Siddhi."

Ito frowned. "Don't endow me with uncanny powers. That's prohibited."

Feeling grumpy, Ito walked away and Masefield followed him.

"So, who's the father?" Masefield asked when they were alone.

"Fuck you," Ito said mildly.

Masefield smiled. "Masef is the father. I know. Because I felt I was the grandfather, as strong as I ever felt anything. Also, he looks like me, don't you think? I felt the generations going on to eternity, Ito. A good feeling. I can die now."

"No you can't. They'd be no one to interfere with Masef's life if you did. No one to find him jobs and kill his girlfriends."

"Fuck you," Masefield said mildly.

It seemed as if Cecile was expecting them. "Come in," she said graciously. Masefield was very interested to see her changed appearance and felt convinced this wasn't the first time she'd created a new identity.

"This is Ito."

She was wearing a kimono which managed to make her appear sexy and convalescent at the same time. "Have you come to see the baby? Everyone is coming to see the baby. But he is with his father now."

"We saw him," Masefield said bluntly, wondering how he could cut through the social jabber and get some things said. Then she surprised him and said some things herself.

"Masef is so devoted to him. I'm glad he is." She sat down on the couch, patting the place next to her, which neither man availed himself of. Nor did they sit elsewhere. Their standing made the room seem crowded.

"It is a great relief to be with a man who has regard for a baby's life and embraces it as his own, even if there is a question of parenthood."

The men stood listening glumly, looking down at this woman portraying herself as a loving mother and wife. She shifted her position, curling her legs under her, looking small and delicate beneath the glum gazes of the powerful men.

"Masef is so unlike Boy. Even though Baby's murder might have been an accident, it was clear to me that Boy had no love for the child I brought to that marriage. No love at all." She took up a tape recorder from the side table and put it in her lap, cradling it. "Masef gives me the courage to go on. And to trust."

She raised her eyes to them. Although she marshalled all her femininity into her glance, she would have gone far to find two more impervious men.

Still, her fluency never wavered, her tone did not falter. "I am in such a frail state from the murders that have happened to those closest to me. I'm so terribly frightened and insecure that sometimes I'm afraid Masef loves the baby too much. More than me. So, when I get too shaky, I play this tape I made. Do you want to hear it?" Careless of their answer, she pressed the button.

"Masef, darling, promise you won't ever leave me."

"I'm not going to leave you, Cecile."

"Then why do you say you won't die with me?"

"Die with you? I thought the idea was to live with you."

"Yes, die if I die, not leave me on my own in the afterlife."

"There is no afterlife. This is it. Live it with all your might."

"I want to make a pact, that if one of us dies, the other will, too. Like Boy's parents."

"No. It's not fair to orphan a kid. It's mean and selfish. Cecile, honey, you're just in a down mood because I went off and left you for the day and it's been a long day. I love you. I'm not going to leave you. All this talk of death and suicide isn't healthy. Let's create a good life for him so he'll grow strong and kind. Anything to eat around here? More importantly, any beer?"

"Promise me you'll kill yourself if I die."

"I promise."

Cecile turned off the tape and smiled victoriously at the two men.

"Very touching," said Masefield dryly, his voice so parched of juice it was more like a croak. "Let's go, Ito."

Laurie fell into step with them a block from the cabin. She was dressed in jeans, jeans jacket, and cowboy hat. Her hair was tucked under it. She looked like a boy. She'd always walked like one.

"Masef doesn't know I'm skulking around here. Don't tell him."

She carried no purse. Her hands were tucked in her back pockets. They were a strange trio: the huge Samoan, the willowy Indian "boy," the long, lean tired white man who looked like a latter-day Abraham Lincoln.

"He's trapped," Masefield said to Ito. "He's in a trap. And I am, too. My hands are tied. If this death pact exists—and I have to admit that the tape is convincing to me—then I can't risk . . . interfering."

"A wily woman," Ito said. "It was as if she had it ready for us to hear, knew her life was at stake."

Masefield told Laurie about the tape.

"I don't believe it," she said. "I believe what he said about not orphaning Buster."

"You don't want to believe it," Masefield said.

"Oh, for Christ's sake, will everybody please just hang up the jealousy angle. It's gone. I don't feel it anymore. I'm cured. Ito, look at me, am I cured?"

"Yes," Ito said, without looking at her.

"See," she said to Masefield. "Ito has insight."

"Speaking of which, Ito, what was your impression of Cecile? Is she a murderer?"

"She is a disturbed person," Ito said.

"Well?"

"You are asking me to judge, but what I have to do is see."

"I understand that."

"I can't see when I am shackled by duelistic thinking—love hate, good bad, right wrong. It creates prejudice, discrimination. I can't see clearly. Everything is disguised."

Masefield nodded.

"There is a Zen monastery here at the foot of Shasta. Let me spend a day or two there, sitting. Maybe I can get my mind right."

"Very well. I'll get a motel room and stick around. We all must do what we must do. What about you, Laurie?"

"I've made camp. I'm not ready to leave either." She told them where it was.

Ito found Shasta Abbey so inhospitable, even oppressive, that he ended by assuming the lotus position at Laurie's camp. Silent and fasting, he sat for twenty-four hours, getting his mind right.

TWENTY-SEVEN

Amy arrived late in the afternoon. The closer she got to Weed the more her spirits lifted. Her heart beat with pleasure and excitement. She would see Masef. She was coming closer and closer to Masef. Even if it was all for naught and he would not come home with her, she would at least see him, look upon his dear face. And if he was happy here in Weed with Cecile, she would try with all her might to let his happiness be her own.

After the twenty-five-hundred-foot tranquil mountain greenery of Tamalpais, which had presided lovingly over her since birth, the mighty snow-covered fastness of Mount Shasta loomed ahead like an admonition. The massive mountain-ness of it was unexpected. It seemed to mount the sky supernaturally, startling and confounding her as it would someone who'd lived on a pond seeing the ocean for the first time and in that awe-ful moment feeling the first creepy, featherweight touch of eternity.

It added to her feeling of excitement. She was traveling. So this is what Masef did those months he'd taken off. What a good idea! So renewing. If he did come home to live with her again and resumed his habit of taking off periodically, maybe she'd go with him instead of waiting. Unless the wanderer needs a waiter in order to wander—and the homebody needs a wanderer to be a waiter for.

After casting about Weed for a half an hour, she found the house and parked in front. It was not the rose-covered cottage of her imagination. It was dingy white and ill formed, a grimy, graceless box. At first, she felt glad. Then she felt sad to think of him living in such a place. Finally, the unsettling thought hit her that he didn't care what his environment was like, that all her housekeeping was for nothing because the only thing that mattered was not where he was, but who he was with. She could clean and decorate the house upside down and sideways and it wouldn't bring him home, or keep him there.

She went to the door and knocked. Masef answered it. He looked at her dumbfounded, much in the way she had just viewed Shasta. Her coming to his door in Weed was as miraculous to him as Mount Tamalpais coming to his door—so rooted to her place was Amy.

And she was dumbfounded, too. He looked so changed. Some grave expression in those violet eyes, something in the way he stood. He looked like Masefield!

Then he swept her into his arms, picking her up off her feet and twirling around, laughing aloud with joy, Amy laughing, too, breathlessly from the strength of his hug. It was all anyone could ask for as a greeting— a greeting to last a lifetime through all the goodbyes to come, even the last.

Then they stood and looked at each other, holding hands. "I don't want to come in," Amy said. "Can you come for a little walk, so that we can talk?"

"Yes. Cecile is resting."

Amy remembered how Cecile seemed always to be

"resting" when she lived with Boy. Amy would wonder what she was resting from. Or for.

"And Buster's sleeping. I'll just ask Boy to watch him for me. Boy's inside. Do you want to say hello?"

"No, I'll wait here."

Masef returned, having donned a blue ski sweater. He shook his head. "I don't know why I ask Boy to watch him when he's the one who wants to take him from me."

"No, he doesn't. He only wants to keep him safe from her."

"I don't believe that accusation, Amy—although I guess I'm beginning to act like I do. This is the first time I've been without the little guy since Laurie told me."

"I think you should believe it."

"Why should I? Boy, himself, doesn't believe it. He asked Cecile to come back to him."

Amy was surprised into silence. She could make nothing of the information. She decided the best course was to ignore it for now. "*I* believe Cecile killed Baby," she said, and then invoked the infallible power, "Masefield does, too."

"Masefield isn't God!"

"He used to be," Amy stammered.

"He's just a person and not even a good person. He's an outlaw. There was a time when I wanted to be like him and then there was a time in which I resigned myself that I never could be. Now I know I don't want to be. I love him. He's a great man. But he's not a good man."

"What's good?"

"I don't know."

As they talked, Masef grew more and more upset, and as he grew more upset his stride lengthened and hastened so that Amy was trotting to keep up with him. "Masef, come home." Tears jumped to her eyes. She couldn't help it.

"I can't," he said.

He said it with such solemnity and certainty that Amy's heart sank. She saw there was no sense in pursuing the subject at all.

But she had left home and come all these miles to ask him to return. She might as well give him the whole message, even though she felt a lot like the messenger who is shot for bringing news that isn't welcome.

"Please come home with me," she said feeling shot, feeling riddled with entry wounds as if being penetrated by her own words as she spoke them. "I miss you. I love you. I've been getting the house all ready for your return."

"Oh, Amy, you're such a one for readying," he said fondly, nostalgically, lovingly, too, she thought.

"It looks so pretty. I imagine you're already there. Sometimes I seem to hear your guitar."

They were still holding hands. He swung their hands back and forth. "I never play guitar anymore," he said sadly. He began to open up to her now, to unburden himseslf. "I was happy with you Amy. I'm not at all happy now. No, not at all."

It hurt Amy to hear this, but she was glad he could talk to her, glad even knowing he could say these things to her only because she understood he was staying with Cecile. "Remember how we'd laugh together, keep bringing up the same old jokes that just kept getting funnier. Cecile and I never laugh, never joke. And it gets worse and worse. I can never leave, not even for a day, without being in for a lot of grief. I get so claustrophobic I want to start yelling my head off. But I can't leave her. The worse it gets, the less able I am to go."

"It just *seems* that way because you're so caught up in it, Masef. Just take Buster and come!"

Even though he'd said he would not come and she believed him, she was pleading.

"No. She needs me too much. What an act of cruelty that would be."

"You left me."

"What?"

"You left me."

"Yes . . . but . . . well, she needed me then, too. More. And I was crazy about her. I'd have done anything."

Now he let go of her hand to put his hands over his face. "Oh, Amy it's so awful. Sometimes I just wish she'd die. I feel like that's the only way I can get free."

"You could get free if you'd just believe us about her," Amy said adamantly. "That would free you in a minute."

He wiped his face on his sleeve and said wearily, "There's nothing to believe, Amy. It's all just talk and feelings."

Amy had to admit that was so. There was no proof. None. And now Boy had asked Cecile back.

They turned and walked back to the house. She wanted to ask, "If she did die, or if you did believe us, would you come home?", but that was just to allow herself to return home and wait and hope and ready, nurture the supportable pain—all to the music of his phantom guitar.

It wasn't a fair question. "If" questions weren't fair.

But one thing she had a right to ask, "How long were you lovers with Cecile?"

"I wasn't. Not until the day of the accident. Amy, go home," he said. He went into the house without a backward glance.

But Amy didn't go home because she'd seen his profound unhappiness. She'd made a vow to him on the night of their first embrace, to love and protect, and she was staunch.

TWENTY-EIGHT

None of us left Weed, although none of us could have said what we were staying for. It was like a dance with different ones coupling off as we circled around and in and out of the house which Cecile herself never left. Ito was at Laurie's camp. Masefield took a motel room. Amy stayed with him. I remained at the house which I considered my "post." Laurie remained distant, rarely seen. At first, only Ito and Masefield knew she was in town, then I found out and told Amy.

We all had conversations together and reported them to each other. Everyone's words were recycled, except Ito's, because he was being silent and Laurie's because none of us saw her.

We all felt apprehensive, waiting for something.

Sometimes I resolved to take Buster and make a run for it. But Masef never left him alone with me again. And what if I did? Masef would just come after me and steal him back.

"But if you did take him," Amy said, "and Masef came for him, maybe he'd stay with us. All he needs is to get away and get some perspective. He's in a tunnel, which is just getting narrower and darker. He can't even see that there are options. I'd say take him. He's *your* child."

Amy had told me what Masef said about not making love to Cecile until the last day.

We were at Masefield's motel room—a separate cottage set in a young fir forest. We sat on the porch. Jays were caterwauling from tree to tree. Shasta, silvery blue in the noonday sun beamed down at us. Amy kept looking at it as if waiting for a message, as if the enormous locked light of its gleaming snowfields would blink on and off in an emergency code.

Masefield, who had brought and installed a conference phone, was inside making a dozen phone calls, trying to keep up with his international life from Weed. Trying and pretty much failing. All over the world, people were angry with him.

I had felt able to abandon my post as Masef had taken Buster for a hike on Shasta.

"She thinks I killed Baby intentionally," I told Amy. "She said I taught her to crawl and then to love the garage door, that I set it all up."

"How hateful of her! You can't teach a baby to crawl, for God's sake! You were just being silly that day."

"What if she's right? She said I never loved Baby and it's true. I didn't."

"She's so evil," Amy said. "I wish she were dead."

"Masefield said that she made Masef promise to kill himself if anything happened to her. He did promise. It's on tape. Masefield heard it."

"Oh God, that's horrible! See how evil she is?"

"She wants their love to be as great as our parents' was."

"Yeah, that was really great."

"She has a lot of power. She makes you do things you would normally never do, just to please her."

"Don't get all enslaved by her again. Masef told me you asked her back."

"I did. God knows how or why, but I did." They

were silent. There was only the sound of the jays and, periodically, Masefield's stern phone voice from the cottage.

"What's really scary is that Cecile is carrying a gun around the whole time now. She says she feels unsafe. Masef says he can see why and sympathizes with her anxiety. More than one of us wishes she was out of the way and have said as much."

"Including Masef," Amy said.

TWENTY-NINE

Laurie crawled out of her sleeping bag, stirred up the ashes, putting dry sticks on the live coals that glimmered in the misty dawn. She added bigger sticks as the little ones blazed up. A lone owl hooted, hanging on to the night. Otherwise, there were only the sounds of crackling fire and of creek water hurrying over pebbles and stones.

Brrr. The fire heat felt nice. She left it to fill the pot with water. Coffee would feel even nicer.

She was glad to see the great mound that was Ito in his sleeping bag. He must have completed his long sit sometime in the night. He must have got his mind right.

She had, too. At least, maybe it wasn't right, but it was made up.

She had completely given up any hope of having a life with Masef, but at least she could create a good life for him before she went away. She could release him from the trap he was in. She had sworn at Buster's grave, when she had the illumination of being a brave, that she would travel this war path to the end. Today was the end.

She had shot plenty of animals. Killing them was nothing to her. This wouldn't be that different. Would it? Yes. She dreaded it with all her heart.

This was a woman. She had to hold tight in her mind that the woman had killed her own child, had ruined Boy and Amy's lives, and now held Masef an emotional prisoner with Baby Buster's life endangered daily.

She wouldn't shirk. Masefield would do it without blinking, except that he believed the tape and that was preventing him from acting. She didn't believe it. She knew Masef better.

She wished she could use her rifle from a distance, but she would have to use Cecile's own gun, which she'd heard was now constantly on her. She would have to get it from her.

Actually, this way was far braver than an ambush. If she must do it, let it at least be hard, let it take courage and nerve, not wile. She embraced her dread.

Ito awoke to the smell of coffee. As he joined Laurie by the fire, he could see by her relaxed features that she'd made some sort of decision.

After a while, they began to talk, Ito saying, "How does it feel to be rid of your fanatical attachment to Masef?"

"I feel free. And yet it's sad, too. I think I only let it go because I gave up all hope. I finally saw and understood that we'd never be together."

"Yes, it is sad. And, until you can feel separate from him and separate from that hope, you won't care about anything. Nothing will seem to matter. You will seem to have nothing to lose because you think you have lost all. And yet, you haven't. You have gained your self and your freedom. Life is beginning for you, Laurie. Try to hold that thought.

Laurie felt chilled by these words because it seemed that Ito, uncannily, had guessed her intention. "But, Ito, life still does matter. I still care about Masef more than anything in the world. I would lay down my life for him. But it's the good love now, unconditional. I don't want anything back. Only his happiness."

Ito shook his head. "He has to find his own happiness. So do you. You can. I have seen you be happy doing simple chores around the camp."

Laurie laughed at his idea of happiness.

"Go away today, Laurie," he said. "Go now."

"But Ito . . ." She lowered her eyes before his look, even though it was so mild, almost dumb. "Okay. I'll go today. Not now, but soon."

THIRTY

That morning, Masef, Cecile and I were hanging around the house. Buster was in his bassinet. Cecile was restless, out of her kimono for once, dressed in slacks and sweater. She paced back and forth. All of a sudden she said, "Boy, why don't you go for a run."

"A run?" I was astonished.

"Yes, don't you think it's high time you started to run again? There's nothing wrong with you as far as I can see. You walked funny when you first arrived, but you seem fine today."

I remembered how I had so longed for her permission to run again, how it would be like an absolution.

But I already had run again. On my own. Without her go-ahead. I'd absolved myself. The re-creation had set me free. Like Ito said.

"Wouldn't you rather run than sit around here? You used to want to run more than anything. You could start a new streak today."

Everything she said was loaded with hatred and vengeance in these references to the obsession that had come between us. Yet, she was right. I vowed I would never again have a streak and never put running before human concerns. I would take a day off every week. Never the same day. I would take a day off whenever the hell I wanted to. My running would not control me. I would not be a fanatic. And maybe I wouldn't be the fastest marathoner in the world, or maybe I would be, but if so, it would not be at the expense of anyone. And I'd run openly and truly, without conniving as I did in Boston.

And I'll help other runners, I vowed to myself. I'll coach! Who knows, maybe I won't have the speed anymore. Or the will. No matter. I'll run for the joy of it, for the freedom and challenge of it.

I stood up. With a flutter in my heart, I spoke the beautiful words, the words that hadn't left my tongue in so very very long: "I think I'll go for a run."

I left them. I did not feel worry at abandoning my post, knowing the others were all around.

After I'd gone, Cecile dragged Masef off to bed and went into a sexual frenzy that left Masef semicomatose on the bed, like a piece of flotsom on a becalmed sea. She, however, bounded to her feet, energized, and quickly dressed. She left the bedroom. Her actions penetrated Masef's befogged brain.

"What are you doing?" Masef asked, alarmed.

No answer. He rolled off the bed, landed on his feet and staggered to the door. She was putting the gun in her jacket pocket. She wore the babypack. She was reaching for Buster.

"I'm going for a walk with my baby," she said.

"I'll go, too. I'll carry him." He grabbed his jeans and stumblingly stepped into them, carefully zipping them over his bare and tender cock. He reached for his shirt and jacket.

"I want to be alone," she said.

"But I *want* to go with you." He paused. Clearly, she abhorred his words. He changed his tack. "Where are you going?"

"Am I allowed to take my own baby for a walk?"

"Sure you are. Of course!"

"This is your chance to show me that you trust me. And you'd better. I'm at the end of my rope."

"I trust you." He did trust her. But he'd been made so nervous by all the others that he didn't know how to act. And Buster had become such a part of him that he felt like he had a limb missing when he wasn't in his arms on in the babypack on his breast.

"Then stop treating me like a prisoner, watching my every move. All of you are watching me. It's driving me crazy. I want you to get Boy to leave today. I know you feel sorry for him and want to be hospitable, but he has no right to be here. If he goes, the others will, too. Otherwise, you will all drive me to do something serious."

Masef felt an escalation of alarm. "But if you feel like that you shouldn't be alone. At least let me take Buster while you have your walk."

"Why?"

"Why, what?" Masef floundered. He stood with his arms reached out for Buster.

"Are you afraid I will hurt this baby?"

If only she would say his name, he moaned to himself. But he had to show that he trusted her. It was crucial to their life together. "No, I am not," he said definitely.

She smiled. "That's good, darling. Why don't you take this opportunity to see your father. He's come all this way and you've scarcely spent any time with him."

Masef put his jacket on. They walked out the door together. He paused. "Please don't take the gun."

"It makes me feel safe. I'll see you later."

Masef watched Cecile walk down the street. He did trust her. *I trust her,* he said to himself. *I do.*

Nevertheless, he was scared as hell to leave her alone with Buster. *Sometimes you can be driven to do the very thing everyone suspects you of,* he thought.

He understood why she thought she needed the gun in order to feel safe, but with all his heart he wished he'd had the strength to take it from her— under any pretext.

He felt terribly upset and confused.

Slowly, he began his walk to Masefield's motel. Suddenly, out of the blue, he had a flashback. The image came before his eyes of her bringing a gun to Baby's death scene. Why? What was a gun doing there as they stood over the dead Baby.

He turned around. Cecile and Buster the Second were still in sight. He stood there, torn, torn, watching her grow smaller in the distance. An Indian boy fell in behind her and cut her off from view. It was Laurie. He'd know her walk anywhere. God almighty! Now Laurie was here, too! He felt a rush of love for her. He knew she would protect Buster. He could go on to see his father and not worry.

He turned and continued on to Masefield's motel. The flashback. Yes, he'd definitely seen her pass Boy the gun, or Boy take the gun from her. Where was she when the accident happened? She said she was lying down resting. But he knew she wasn't.

Because they'd had sex together that very morning. They'd had sex together in his and Amy's bed. How low can you get? Being unfaithful to both Boy and Amy, and in Amy's own bed. Amy was in the darkroom, but could return at any time. Boy was doing chores and they could hear him talking to Baby as he went to and fro. It was completely nervewracking and maniacally exciting. He was sitting groggily at the edge of his bed when she entered. He was naked and in a minute she was too. She was sitting on his erect penis with her legs around his waist and putting her breast in his mouth.

Boy was doing his chores. Amy was in the darkroom. Any minute he might hear their steps on the boardwalk connecting the houses. Boy would knock, but Amy wouldn't.

He'd been hanging around Cecile for days, wanting her so bad, feeling hopelessly hot, a pitiable creature in his longing for any kindness from her, any touch. She knew it. She invited and repulsed him at the same time, mostly repulsed him. Now, here she was sitting on him and he was deep into her burning center groaning his head off, her insides wrapped around him. She was like a whirling dervish. When he came, he gripped her ass so hard she had black and blue finger marks for days. He toppled back down. It was like a frenzy.

It was like today.

And then what? Then she was gone and he hopped into the shower. When he turned it off, he heard the garage door go up. The garage was connected to the cottage. So when she left him it was maybe only five minutes before the accident, according to Laurie's retelling of it to him at her campsite near Buster's grave. Maybe less. He heard Boy moving stuff around in the garage and then starting the car. By then, Amy had come into the cottage and was washing her hands at their bathroom sink while he towelled himself dry, knowing he'd have to tell Amy about him and Cecile, the sooner the better.

Then they heard Boy scream. And life turned into hell for them all.

"She could have left your bed and seen Boy exiting the house with the bucket," Masefield said when Masef told him how the flashback had recalled forgotten details of that fatal day.

They were sitting on the twin beds in the motel room. "She could have watched Boy go the garage for the car, and seized the moment to get Baby from the lawn and put her on the drive."

"We'll never know," Masef moaned. "We'll never know." He was literally wringing his hands. "I have to believe her. That's all I can do."

"Believe her if you must. But leave her. Will you leave her now?" All of his father-love for him was in his face and Masef thought, *how could I have told Amy he was not a good man. He is a prince. He has always been the most loving father in the world. It's I who have been the crummy son, never doing what he wants, even now . . .*

Masefield lit a cigarette. He smoked with no pleasure. *Has he always been this thin?* Masef wondered. *He should take a break. Go home and be with Sunny. Just be.*

"Even the *chance* of her being a murderess is reason enough for you to cut out," Masefield said.

"No," said Masef. "I'll have to confront her. I can't leave without talking to her about it, hearing her side. In any case, I can't possibly leave without Buster. And if I took him, it would kill her!" He could see the scene so well in his mind that he already was defeated. Masef felt wretched. He wished he could think of a joke. He got up to get a glass of water to do something with his hands besides wring them.

"If you confront her, she'll trap you. She'll entangle you into her psyche. Just go. Take Buster and go."

"That's what Amy says." The glass of water trembled. He used both hands to raise it to his mouth. "But leaving without confronting her would be bailing out. It's unheroic, Dad. You can understand that. It wouldn't solve anything or teach anything. Even being in danger isn't reason to leave. Less reason because it makes it more unheroic."

Masefield thought, *she has to be stopped. It isn't enough for him to leave her because there'll be other men, other babies.*

"Cecile told me you'd made a death pact with her. Promise me you won't ever kill yourself because of her."

Masef laughed. He could hear the slight hysterical note in the sound that came from his throat. "Am I to make a pact with you . . ."

"A promise will do."

"No, Dad. And I won't stand by and let her be hurt. I want you all to go home and let me work things out for myself."

Ito had followed Laurie to Cecile's, seen Cecile and Masef part company on the road and Laurie tail after Cecile. Now he joined the parade, eventually coming abreast of Laurie. "Everything's under control," he told her. "Go away. Trust me."

Laurie drifted away.

Ito then caught up to Cecile. He asked for the gun, which he had heard she constantly carried. She refused to give it to him and said she wanted to be alone. It was a simple matter for Ito to dispossess her of the weapon because, unlike Masef, he wasn't afraid for her to think he didn't trust her. They walked along silently, Cecile pale with anger, but as time passed she seemed to relax and even enjoy the walk.

An hour later, when they were back at the house,

Ito took Buster out of the babypack and into his arms. "I'll wait outside for Masef," he explained.

She asked for the gun and he gave it back to her. "I understand that you're frightened," he said kindly. Buster began to cry. Ito saw how it made no impression on her.

"I am frightened," she said. "No one likes me. You all want me out of the way. The angel of death follows me everywhere," she said dramatically, but Ito heard pain as well.

She seemed to feel the depth of his look. "I trust you," she said. "You are the only one."

Ito asked, "Why do you say that Boy killed Baby?"

"I never said he meant to. But I blamed him. When I saw Baby crushed to death, I wanted him to die, too. I wanted to kill him. I'd already started to hate him, anyhow. But he took the gun away from me. I thought he would kill himself, but he didn't. He should have been willing to die. There are times when people should die. If you lose a baby's life through carelessness, you should be willing to kill yourself on the spot. Masef would."

Ito said, "That's why we're all so frightened that something will happen to Buster."

"Nothing will happen," she said. "Because Masef loves Buster and loves me. Boy didn't love Baby and he loved his running more than me." Her face grew pale and still as it had been earlier on the walk, like a death mask. "But now you're all poisoning Masef against me." Abruptly she turned and entered the house.

Ito began to walk up and down the street to calm little Baby Buster the Second whose cries, during their exchange, had grown more desperate.

A half hour later, Masef returned. As Ito passed

him the baby, Boy rounded the corner, running, looking happy.

The three men went into the house together. They all found the body together.

THIRTY-ONE

Cecile was dead and I was free. Free and absolved.

Everyone was free, but I was the absolved one. I would run again professionally. There was still time for me to get in shape for the Olympic trials' marathon. I knew I could do it. And if it came up, in an interview or anything, about Baby's death, I would tell the world in effect, what we all had come to believe, that Cecile had murdered her child herself and, within the year, taken her own life because of it.

I had found it impossible to believe. I was the last to believe it. But now that she was dead, I did believe it. Yes, she had put Baby beneath the wheel, beneath where the wheel would come, picked Baby up from wherever she was lying at the time and put her in the driveway in the course of the killer car. I could go on in a living death and that would be fine with her. If I shot myself, all the better.

I didn't mourn her at all. No. It seemed like her death had freed me in other ways, too, to be angry, to stop loving her, to acknowledge her cruelty.

I didn't even stay for the burial. I sold the old Volvo up in Shasta City and drove on home with Amy, who didn't care about staying either.

On the drive back, I planned how to get Buster. "Of course, if Masef comes back to you," I told Amy, "that will solve everything. We can all three live together like we used to. Only now it will be four. We can all raise the little guy together. I'd be willing to do that, Amy, wouldn't you?"

"What if you fall in love again, Boy? Then what would happen?"

"I'm through with love. I've got my kid and there's no reason to love again. It's just going to be me and you and running. And Buster."

"I don't know. Masef didn't say anything about us being together. I know he's going to take Buster home to Inverness and Sunny. Masefield's going, too. Masef said he'd be in touch. That doesn't sound much like will you marry me."

"He can hardly ask you with Cecile fresh in her grave."

"The grave wither we goest . . ."

"What?"

"Nothing." Amy sighed. "We hounded that woman to her grave."

"Maybe so. But that's why we all went to Weed. To save Buster and Masef. And we did. And I'm glad. I'm glad she's dead. Everyone is."

"What if Masef doesn't come back to us?"

"Buster's my son. There are blood tests . . ."

"But you wouldn't take Masef to court to force him to give Buster up, would you?"

"Maybe. I don't know. We'll see. We'll take it a step at a time. Maybe Ito could decide. Maybe we could put it into Ito's hand's. I'd abide by a decision of his."

When we arrived home, the house looked beautiful. How many people in the world had such a house? I was feeling so lucky, now, so happy. Everything was going to be great. A hundred albatrosses had been lifted from my neck.

But, strangely, Amy, looking at the house she loved even more than I did, said, "I feel like I should just keep on going, that if I go in the house, I'll never come out. I'll be there the rest of my days. It's a beautiful house, Boy, but not a happy house, not a lucky house. Tell me to keep on going."

"Hell, no. It's you and me together, forever. The orphans. One time Cecile told me to ask you to go. I said never in a million years."

"I could still keep on going," Amy said. But she didn't.

Masefield and Ito left Weed, Ito to return to his wife and child in Stinson Beach, Masefield to Washington to wind up his affairs. Then he was going home to Inverness for a long break to be with Sunny. He was tired.

At parting, Ito said to him, "You never asked me again what I saw in Cecile's heart."

When Masefield said nothing, Ito said, "You don't want to know, do you?"

"You're right, my friend." Masefield put a weary hand on Ito's outrigger of a shoulder. "All I know or care about is that Masef is safe."

"Life is impermanent," Ito said. "Tonight, tomorrow morning, any one of us can meet any kind of death."

Laurie stayed in Weed with Masef and Buster, and to see Cecile buried. Her family didn't come.

Afterward, she helped Masef clean the little house, give away Cecile's effects, pack up his own few things with the baby clothes and gear for Buster. It was while they were packing, Laurie said, "I took Mom's car to come up here when I followed you. You can have it to take back to Inverness. No way you can hitch with all this stuff and Baby Buster, too."

"What do you mean? Aren't you coming back?"

"No, I'm moving on."

"I don't get it."

"I think I'll go on up to Canada. There must be work for an Indian brave up there. Great thing about my business is that wherever you go there's junk to haul. People just don't like hauling their own trash. Don't seem to see the fun of it."

"Laurie, I don't want you to go. I want you to stay with me."

"Stay with you, M?" A look of something like panic came to her eyes. A hand flew to her throat.

"Yes. Let's go back home and raise up Buster together."

Tears burst out of Laurie's eyes. She grabbed one of Buster's undershirts and wiped them away. "I can't," she said. "No."

"What do you mean, you can't? Hey, Laurie, it's me, Masef, the love of your life. At least that's what you always told me."

"I know who it is."

"Well, what's the deal? I'm not just asking you to help us. I want to live together and love each other with all our might, like you always said we would. Marry me!" He smiled, almost shyly. "I asked Ito if I could go to work for him as assistant gardener. He said yes."

All emotion left her and she said stolidly, the words dropping from her mouth like stones, "You should marry Amy. She loves you. You were happy with her. She'll be a good mother. She's the one."

"I can't believe I'm hearing this. I thought this was what you always wanted. Now I want it, too." He was quiet a minute, looking at Laurie's unflinching face. Then he said seriously, "On the day of . . . of Cecile's death, I saw you tagging along with her and Buster, looking out for him. I hadn't known you were here. I realized you hadn't come to hound Cecile, but just to guard Buster and I felt so much love for you. Then I knew that if I could get away from Cecile, I'd go to you . . . not Amy. Yes, I was happy with Amy but . . . I couldn't be sad with her. Then I had to get away by myself, or spend a little time with you."

Laurie cracked and let out a sound like a howl. "Stop it! I'm going. Goodbye." She thrust the little undershirt in her pocket, taking it with her.

He followed her to the door. Now his face was panicked and unhappy. It was her turn to wheel around and say, "Don't follow me."

It was more than a month later that Masef showed up at Amy's house. She flew into his arms. "Oh, Masef, at last! I'm so happy to see you. I knew you had to have a time to grieve, but I was beginning to think it would never end. Where's Buster?"

"He's home with Sunny. Masefield's there, too. I can't believe the man's actually taking a vacation. He's probably disappointed as hell to realize civilization can go on without him, that governments aren't falling all over the world."

Amy laughed. She spread her arms. "Come in, come in. Do you want anything. A beer . . . ?

"No, nothing. And I don't want to come in. Let's sit out in the yard. Is Boy around?" he asked, flinging himself down on the lounge.

"No, he's running. He's getting fit again fast," she

laughed, "and has a new streak going, too. I think he's going to do it. He'll run in the Olympic trials and then I think he'll go to the Olympics. I'm so proud of him. What a comeback. I'm so glad . . . it all turned out . . ." She flushed.

"I know." Masef frowned. "It's only too bad it was at the expense of a life."

"Don't you think that justice was done?"

"No, I don't. Maybe she wasn't a good mother. Maybe she wasn't a good person. But she wasn't a murderer." He added direly, "I don't think she was a suicider, either."

Amy flushed again. "Do you mean it? You don't think Cecile killed herself? But she was always threatening to. Maybe you just want to think she was murdered because of the pact, because you feel you let her down about the pact?"

"No, the pact was all crap. I never meant I'd die if she did and she knew I didn't. She just needed to hear me say it. I don't believe she'd take her life. There was no reason for her to. I've been thinking a lot about it. Granted, she was depressed and everyone was driving her nuts hovering around. But at the same time, she liked the attention. She liked being the center of things, causing drama. That was her thing in life. If anything, you all coming to Weed picked her up, gave her a boost, made her feel important."

"Masefield would know," Amy said certainly. "If there was anything in the least funny about her death, he'd know. Did you ask him?"

"Yeah, he'd know all right, but he wouldn't say. He finds out, but then he decides who else, if anyone, should get to know too. He plays God. But he told me one thing, which is that there's no proof Cecile was ever married, let alone that her husband was shot."

They were quiet. He closed his eyes and lifted his face to the sun. "Masef?"

"Yeah?"

She drew a deep breath and forced out the words with the exhale. "You're not coming back here, are you?"

He opened his eyes and looked at her directly. "No, Amy, I'm not. It isn't to do with you. It's Boy. I don't want to live with Boy."

"Because of Baby Buster?"

"No, because I don't like him."

Amy bent her head. This was very hard to hear. It hurt her. Boy was such a part of her. He might as well say he didn't like her. After a while, she asked, "Where's Laurie?"

"Laurie took off. Up to Canada. It's the first time she's gone out of my life. That I haven't known where she is, that I can't go to her if I need to."

"All the times you thought she was so afraid to lose you, it was really the other way around."

"I guess it was both ways."

"She was the woman you always loved."

"Yeah, funny I could say it but not know it. Now I know it."

Amy bent her head again, as if to a guillotine.

"I'm sorry if I'm hurting you again, hurting you more, but I have to tell you that I asked Laurie to come live with me. I asked her to marry me."

This was so painful, so unbearably hard to hear that she almost shut down. Instead, as so often happens when you hit emotional bottom, she began to feel liberated.

"She said no."

Amy stammered. "But that's so amazing. Why?"

"She said I should be with you?"

"Laurie? Said that?"

"If, knowing my feelings, you still want to be with me, you're welcome. I know we can be happy together. We've proved that. But there are scars now that weren't there before. And our life cannot include Boy. You'd have to give up Boy. And the house. I know that's a lot to ask. It's a huge amount to ask. Especially after what I've just told you."

Oh, how she wanted to live with Masef again and be Buster's mother. But she remembered how Boy had been asked to send her away, and he'd said never in a million years. Should she give up Boy and the house for this man she loved, but who didn't love her the same way, who had left her once for another, and who right now wanted to be with someone else? Plus, there was still the question of who's child Buster was.

"I'll have to think, Masef. I'll have to think it over."

"Fair enough. I want to make up to you the hurt I did. I don't think you see Boy for what he is. He doesn't love you as much as you suppose. And if he wants Buster, it's only because he thinks Buster's his, not because he loves him."

Amy said softly. "I think Cecile corrupted your mind against Boy."

"Maybe so. But I lived with Cecile eight months. I knew her best. She was a seductress, not a lover. She was disturbed as all hell, maybe nuts. But she wasn't a killer. In a way, she was too helpless to be one. She had absolutely no energy. Well . . ." he considered, "except sexual . . ."

"The passive-seeming person, the depressed person, is often full of anger and hostility," Amy said.

"I know." Masef's face grew long, remembering his time with Cecile. What a nightmare. But out of it had come his precious child, his fatherhood.

He got up from the lounge and they walked to his car together. "I hope you decide to come, Amy."

THIRTY-TWO

Almost another month went by before I announced to Amy that I'd asked Ito to come over to give me advice on what to do about Buster. "I said I'd abide by his decision. If he says Buster is Masef's, I'll believe him. Ito will know."

"Why do you want Buster so much, Boy?"

"Because if he's my kid, he should be with me. I'm not going to do to him what my parents did to me." Even as I said that I knew there was no analogy. Still, Masef was a loser and couldn't give the kid any kind of stable life. Amy and I could.

Ito came. He didn't embrace us, just sort of bowed. He looked wonderful. I hadn't seen him since Weed. He was very calm, very present.

We sat around the dining room table. The mountain looked in on us.

He said, with no particular emphasis. "Little Baby Buster the Second is Masef's son."

I was stunned. I jumped up scraping back the chair. "How could you say that? It's not true. You of all people, not to see the truth!"

"It is you who are without truth," Ito said. "You suckered us all."

At first I thought he meant succoured as in saved and helped. He turned his clear gaze on me. I felt it penetrate my heart and soul. "Ito, I never said she killed Baby. I never once said it. It was you and Masefield who deduced it from . . . from . . ."

"The re-creation," said Ito.

"Yes."

Ito was silent.

"Don't you believe me?"

"I believe it was an accident. You put Baby down, and Baby crawled on to the driveway. But *where* did you put her down. Was it the place you put Amy in the re-creation?"

"It might not have been in the exact place."

"It wasn't anywhere near. The truth was, you put baby right near the driveway where she could watch the garage door and she crawled out onto the gravel."

"But," I cried, "I knew she couldn't crawl even that far. She couldn't crawl at all!" I was talking loudly. I couldn't control my voice. "She was such a lump," I shouted. "I never meant for her to be killed. Never!"

"I know." Ito lowered his eyes, sad and silent.

"But Boy," Amy asked. Her voice quavered, then hardened. "Why did you lie?"

I began to pace as I talked, moving woodenly, as if my old disease were coming back to me, stumping around the silent sad man, answering Amy to him. "I wanted to be absolved. I wanted to run again. I didn't mean to make it look like Cecile had done it. But somehow, for some reason, in the re-creation, involuntarily, I put Baby down really far away. I couldn't help myself. And then, I believed it. Because I felt so happy."

"But why didn't you stop us when we all began to accuse Cecile?" Amy persisted. She looked horrified.

"Because I thought it could be true. She *could* have come and moved Baby. She *could* have impulsively stuck her there when she saw the bucket of water, knowing I was about to pull the car out. She didn't love the kid at all. Not at all. I *wanted* it to be true that she'd killed her. I was willing to let it be. So I could run. And then, when I saw her in Weed, I wanted her back, especially knowing she had my son. I thought that would absolve me even more, if she came back."

"But she wouldn't come," Ito said, looking at me again, holding me with his gaze so that my pacing stopped and I almost felt peaceful because I knew, no matter what, he would still love me.

"She is just as dead as if you shot her yourself," Amy said relentlessly. "You have to face up to it, Boy. You killed her with the lie."

I hung my head. Were they right? Did my altering of the story cause Cecile's death? Couldn't she still be a murderess no matter where I put Baby, no matter where I said I put her? She was a terrible woman. And here I was, ready to take the Gold for America, which only two marathoners have done in the hundred years. I honestly didn't feel I had anything to face up to. I had suffered and I had prevailed. But I couldn't bear for Ito to think ill of me. I'd give up Buster if he said so, if he would only still love me and let me run.

"Will you still love me?" I asked him.

"Yes," he said, as I knew he would, but it was not like that long ago day when he hugged me and gave me his two blessings. He stood up and, without touching me at all, without looking at me again, walked out of the room and the house.

"He still loves me," I told Amy. "He still believes in me."

"But only because he loves everyone," Amy said, wiping her wet face. "That's the only reason. It's his religion. He's a priest. He has to love us."

"No, Amy, not because he has to, because he's *able* to." Still, I felt scared, feeling that Ito had abandoned me. "Amy, you won't leave me because of this, will you?"

Amy looked at me, then her eyes drifted around the house, as if looking for something, maybe a way out. "Cecile died because of you, Boy. Baby did too."

"It was only a lie," I said.

"What about Trueboy? Where is he?"

"He never was. I never knew what truth was. I still don't. The only thing I know about and understand and care about, is running."

"Well, you've got your running. And, so that Masef and Buster could be safe from the person we believed her to be, Cecile got murdered."

THIRTY-THREE

Laurie didn't go to Canada to haul trash. She went to Montana, Blackfoot country, to her tribe. She decided she'd stay a while with with her original people. Then, in time, maybe she'd move on, maybe she wouldn't. It was going to be desperately hard to be so far away from M and Buster. But what else could she do? If she'd stayed, she'd have benefited. She couldn't benefit or the act would be tainted, impure. In a way, she had given her life for M.

Around her neck she wore a bead necklace that supported a small leather pouch. In the pouch was a scrap of Buster's undershirt. It was her talisman.

All she could hope was that enough years would pass that one morning, she'd wake up and know it was okay, enough time had gone by that she could return. Masef would be married to Amy and have more children. He'd probably be in the landscaping business. Mostly he'd be being a father.

Maybe, she thought, if by then I've survived all the years of lonliness and isolation, all the months of howling at the moon, and if I haven't turned into a drunk or a crazy, then I can go home.

Maybe M will want me to be part of the family, want the kids to know me. Maybe he'll let me stay.

One day Amy showed up on Masef's doorstep. He was sitting on it, playing his guitar to Buster who was in a playpen in the yard. Amy thought the long gangling figure, in blue jeans and blue work shirt, crouched over the guitar, looked like an early Picasso painting—except for the background.

It was a small house in Point Reyes Station—pale yellow, set near an inlet to Tomales Bay. Buster the First had lived there and left it to M when he died.

"I've come," Amy said, putting down her duffel bag in the glorious snarl of wild grasses and flowers that made up the yard. Masef put aside his guitar, rose to his feet, smiling. "I've left the house and Boy," she said. Hearing his name, Masef's face clouded. She knew he'd learned about the lie. "He'll be going to the trials. He's a driven man . . ." Amy felt like she was making a speech, a defense, but she had to get it out of the way. "Such a talent as he has is a terrible burden. It made him lie. And so, Cecile died."

Worse, so much worse, she believed it had made one of them kill, but she would not speak of that.

She smiled lovingly. "But I'm not here because I don't want to be with Boy. I'm following my heart."

"I'm glad you've come." Masef was standing next to her now. He leaned down and kissed her. It was more like a blessing than a salutation. It was lovely. "Buster's glad, too," he said smiling.

Amy went to the playpen and lifted Buster the Second into her arms, kissing him. He was a child of light. Masef put his arms around them both. "I've been thinking so much about Laurie," Amy said, because there was one more thing she had to say before beginning their life together. "Have you heard anything from her?"

"No. And I don't think I will for a long time."

Amy searched his face. She figured he'd come to the same conclusion she had. "Masef, I think one day she'll come home, she'll just appear. And," Amy said, vowing, "we'll ask her to stay. We'll ask her to be part of the family."

THIRTY-FOUR

I won the trials easily. No one called me. I guess none of them watched. When I got home: no party, no flowers on the tables, no Amy. Still the mountain, though.

It's okay. I honestly don't care. I'm an Olympian. I'm going to get the record. Maybe someday, after I'm gone, they'll tell Buster his father was the fastest marathoner the world has ever known.